Baron Bunsen

Prayers

Anatiposi

Baron Bunsen

Prayers

Reprint of the original, first published in 1871.

1st Edition 2023 | ISBN: 978-3-38211-211-0

Anatiposi Verlag is an imprint of Outlook Verlagsgesellschaft mbH.

Verlag (Publisher): Outlook Verlag GmbH, Zeilweg 44, 60439 Frankfurt, Deutschland
Vertretungsberechtigt (Authorized to represent): E. Roepke, Zeilweg 44, 60439 Frankfurt, Deutschland
Druck (Print): Books on Demand GmbH, In de Tarpen 42, 22848 Norderstedt, Deutschland

PRAYERS

FROM THE COLLECTION OF THE LATE

BARON BUNSEN.

PART I.

For the Family.

'Where two or three are gathered together in my name, there am I in the midst of them.'

PART II.

Prayers and Meditations for Private Use.

'Enter into thy closet, and when thou hast shut thy door, pray unto thy Father which is in secret.'

SELECTED AND TRANSLATED BY

CATHERINE WINKWORTH.

LONDON:
LONGMANS, GREEN, AND CO.
1871.

PREFACE.

ALL READERS of Bunsen's *Life* or writings must be aware of the deep and constant interest he took in that branch of literature which gives voice to the common sentiment of Christian people in the worship of God—in liturgies, prayers, and hymns. His love of historical investigation, and the strong bent of his mind towards the discovery of the principle which unites, amid the diversity and apparent conflict of beliefs, alike led him to devote no inconsiderable portion of his time and efforts to researches in this direction. He recognised clearly the necessity in these days that our reformed Christianity should penetrate not merely the life of man as an individual, but also his life as a nation and race. Hence he valued whatever bore witness to the historical manifestation and unity of religion in the past; and also believed that a present basis of union might be found in a common liturgy and common action for purposes of charity and mercy, by men who might be little able to agree in any intellectual propositions concerning the objects of faith, beyond those simple and fundamental ones which underlie all Christian worship. The results of these researches are scattered through his works, but are collected in his *Hippolytus*, and in his *Evangelical Hymn and Prayer-Book*. It is from this last collection that the prayers composing the present work are chosen. It was originally published in 1832, in a large volume containing as many as nine hundred and thirty hymns, and three hundred and fifty prayers. Some years later an abridged edition was brought out in a more manageable compass. This contains, besides hymns adapted for the congregation and about two hundred and fifty prayers designed for private or family use, a complete liturgy for the German Evangelical Church, compiled from a great variety of ancient and modern sources, but in its general features closely resembling our own Common Prayer. Some of the collects and one or two prayers in the present work are taken from this liturgy; the rest are from the collection intended for use at home.

The arrangement into prayers for the mornings and evenings of three weeks, as well as the distinction made between those adapted to household or to individual devotion, is my own, and is designed to facilitate the practical employment of the book. Most of the prayers appropriate to the ordinary current of life—prayers of praise and thanksgiving for its daily joys, of earnest desire for guidance and strength amid its daily cares and toils—have naturally found their place in the First Part of this volume, though many of them are as suitable for individual as for family use. Those in the Second Part deal chiefly with special states of feeling, or the more private emotions of aspiration, sorrow, and penitence.

To nearly all the prayers the name of the author and the date of his life are affixed. In those taken from ancient sources I have followed Bunsen's German text; one long meditation by St. Jerome has been slightly abridged by the omission of a few sentences almost entirely made up of quotations from Scripture; but with this exception I have adhered strictly to the form given by Bunsen. The meditations bearing the name of St. Augustine are derived from certain treatises—the *Meditationes*, *Soliloquia*, and *Manuale*—which were formerly attributed to him, and are still included as an appendix in editions of his collected works. They are, however, considered to be of much later date, and of uncertain authorship, and are composed of a few passages from the authentic writings of St. Augustine, and many more from those of St. Anselm, St. Bernard, Hugo of St. Victor, and others, woven into a continuous whole. But as Bunsen's German work follows the common practice of calling them by St. Augustine's name, it has been retained in the present volume.

With regard to the prayers composed by later German divines, I have been somewhat less scrupulous in adhering to the original form. Where the prayer seemed appropriate to use in the family, but was written throughout with the singular pronoun, the 'I' has been changed into 'we;' and in other instances my version has been abridged in order to bring it within serviceable limits. Many of these prayers, though full of deep and true devotion, are disfigured by prolixity, repetitions, and the tendency to fall into long catalogues of blessings or of persons to be prayed for. These have been curtailed, but in all other respects I have endeavoured faithfully to preserve both the spirit and style of the originals. And many have needed no change whatever; the prayers of Tersteegen (with the exception of one or two redundant sentences) are given exactly as they stand in Bunsen's book. Those of Stark have been only very slightly abridged in a few cases, and 'we' substituted for 'I;' while those of Lassenius have needed much condensation.

We have so many manuals of devotion already existing among us that it may seem scarcely necessary to add another to their number; but good prayers, like hymns, will justify themselves by finding their own way to the hearts that want them, and adding one fresh witness, however small, to the real communion of saints in all ages and lands.

C. W.

CLIFTON: *June* 3, 1871.

CONTENTS.

PART I.

Prayers for the Family.

PART II.

Prayers and Meditations for Private Use.

PRAYERS.

PART I.

For the Family.

"Where two or three are gathered together in my name, there am I in the midst of them."

THE LORD'S PRAYER.

Our Father which art in heaven, hallowed be Thy Name. Thy kingdom come. Thy will be done in earth as it is in heaven. Give us this day our daily bread. And forgive us our trespasses, as we forgive them that trespass against us. And lead us not into temptation; but deliver us from evil. For Thine is the kingdom, and the power, and the glory, for ever and ever. Amen.

The grace of our Lord Jesus Christ, and the love of God, and the fellowship of the Holy Ghost, be with us all evermore. Amen.

Thou our eyes, and we shall behold wondrous things out of Thy law. For Thou only art wise, and to Thee be all honour, through Jesus Christ our Lord, for ever and ever. Amen.

Albinus, 1652.

Sunday Evening.

ABIDE with us, O Lord, for the day is far spent and the night is at hand! O living God, how unsearchable are Thy works, how unspeakable is the goodness which Thou showest to the children of men! We must speak of Thy mercy and truth, for in this day that is gone Thou hast been bountiful to us in body and soul. Thou hast fed our souls with the bread of life, and given us to drink of living waters; Thy Word is sweeter than honey and the honeycomb. May it henceforth be a light unto our path, so that we may guide our conduct by it, and fall not into sin and error on our way. Thou hast cared for us also in earthly things, so that we have reached this evening in health and peace. We are not worthy of all Thy blessings. But now, Our Guardian, let Thy protection be round about us; let Thy light shine continually within us, that we may have no fellowship with the unfruitful works of darkness. Let the Word we have heard be as good seed in our hearts, bringing forth in us fruits that all men may see,—the fear and love of God, and deadness to the world and sin. When we return to our daily toil be our Shield against the arrows of temptation, our Shelter in the heat of the day. The Lord is the strength of our life, of whom then shall we be afraid? Avert all perils of the night from our house; let all the sad, the sick, the dying, enjoy Thy gracious presence to-night. Forgive us if we have not worshipped Thee to-day with as much ardour as we ought, and take not away Thy grace from us. Let all things be new with us in this new week; give us new love and desire for Thee; new zeal to serve and obey Thee; let us avoid and flee from the sins we have committed in the week that is past, that all may know that our Sunday has not been spent in vain. Help us to remember that we have never-dying souls, that we may be more concerned for them than for our perishable bodies. We are about to seek our place of repose; let it remind us not only of the slumber of the grave, but of that rest which Thou hast prepared for the people of God. For that rest do Thou make us meet; strengthen and quicken us, and bring us thither in Thine own time, for Thy mercy's sake. Amen.

Stark, 1740.

Monday Morning.

O THOU loving and merciful God, we are now beginning a new week under Thy protection. We know not what may happen to us in the course of it; how much joy or sorrow one day may bring forth, how much more the whole week. Therefore at its very outset we draw near to Thee, and commend ourselves wholly into Thy hands. Give us, O God, Thy Holy Spirit, to purify, govern, and guide us, and to bear witness within us that we are children of God. Bless this week to us; bless our coming in and going out, our occupations and the business to which Thou hast called us. We lift our eyes unto the hills, from whence cometh our help; even from Thee, O Lord, who hast made heaven and earth. If Thou guide us, we shall not go astray; if Thou uphold us, we shall not fall; therefore let Thy mercy and goodness be ever around us. Bless whatsoever is ours, and let it prosper to Thy praise.

O faithful Father, keep and defend us from hurt and danger, loss and disaster; let us dwell day and night in Thy favour and grace. Guard our home; be Thou a strong wall to us and those whom we love, so shall we not be utterly cast down whatever misfortune may overtake us. Hear us when we cry to Thee in any emergency, and let us not go unanswered from the throne of grace. Keep us, O Lord, from sin; show us Thy ways and guide us in Thy truth. Unite our hearts to fear Thy Name; let that holy fear be so deep within us that we may never turn away from Thee, but continue in Thy grace to our life's end. Grant that this week we may grow more God-fearing and holy, may increase in the knowledge and love of Thee, and add to our faith virtue, to virtue modesty, to modesty temperance, to temperance patience, and to patience joy in the Lord. But if this coming week should be spent beneath the shadow of the cross, O send to us the Comforter, and may He strengthen us with might to endure and overcome all things. Be Thou our help and refuge in every trouble.

Now we commit ourselves, with all we have and all we love, unto Thy fatherly care, and not ourselves only but all our fellow-Christians. Be Thou gracious to us all, and show Thyself, what indeed Thou art, the Saviour of all men, but especially of them that put their trust in Thee. For Thy dear Son's sake. Amen.

Stark, 1740.

Monday Evening.

COLLECT.

PRAISED be Thou, O God, Almighty Ruler, who dost make the day bright with Thy sunshine, and the night with the beams of heavenly fires; who hast led us through the hours of daylight and hast brought us to the quiet night! Listen now to our prayers, and the prayers of Thy whole people, and forgive us all both our conscious and unconscious transgressions. Accept our evening sacrifice, and pour out upon us, Thy heritage, the fullness of Thy mercy and Thy compassions. Protect us by Thy holy angels; clothe us with the armour of righteousness; shield us with Thy truth; watch over us with Thy power; save us from all calamity, and from the snares of our adversaries; and give us grace to pass this evening and night, and all the days of our life, blameless, holy, peaceful, free from sin, terror, and offence. For with Thee is mercy and plenteous redemption, O Lord Jesu Christ, our Lord and God, and to Thee we bring our thanks and praise. Amen.

Greek Church.

PRAYER.

O FATHER of Lights, how much cause have we to thank Thee for the many benefits which Thou hast showered to-day on us and ours, on all Thy people, yea, on the whole world! Every blessing Thou hast given is a fresh testimony to Thy overflowing love towards us, who are so far beneath Thee. Thy gifts, O God, are one with Thy love, as the warmth is with the light. Therefore we love Thee the Giver, and also the gifts which are the instances of Thy love; and our lips praise Thee. O that every complaint of ours, every cry of impatience, might be changed into a song of thankfulness; for even when Thou tarriest with Thy help, yet is this very delay a true kindness, teaching us to pray, to seek, to knock more earnestly, and to wait in patience upon Thy all-wise Providence. So now this night we ask Thy presence among us, O Lord Jesus; when our bodies sleep may our souls rest in Thee; to Thy loving heart, O great High Priest, we commend ourselves and all whom we love, our friends and also our foes; and most especially those who have asked us to remember them in our weak intercessions. Plead Thou for them and for us evermore. Amen.

Storr, 1756.

Tuesday Morning.

COLLECT.

O LORD our God, holy and incomprehensible, who hast bidden the light to shine out of darkness, who hast refreshed us by nightly slumbers, and again wakened us to praise Thy goodness and ask for Thy grace: accept now, in Thy endless mercy, the sacrifice of our worship and thanksgiving, and grant unto us all such requests as may be wholesome for us. Make us to be children of the light and of the day, and heirs of Thy everlasting inheritance. Remember, O Lord, according to the multitude of Thy mercies, Thy whole Church; all who join with us in prayer; all our brethren by land or sea, or wherever they may be in Thy vast kingdom, who stand in need of Thy grace and succour. Pour out upon them the riches of Thy mercy, so that we, redeemed in soul and body, and steadfast in faith, may ever praise Thy wonderful and holy name. Amen.

Greek Church.

PRAYER.

O LORD our God, we thank Thee with our whole hearts that Thou hast so mercifully preserved us through the past night, and suffered us to meet again this morning at Thy throne safe and well, an unbroken family. We humbly beseech Thee to forgive us whatever was amiss in the hours that have just fled, and to keep us this day, with all that is ours, and all who are dear to us, in Thy Divine protection. Do Thou, who art the Light of all men, so dwell in our hearts that our mind and conscience may be enlightened, that we may grow from day to day in the knowledge of Thy holy will, and learn to walk honestly, as becometh the day; not in covetousness, or in wantonness, in ambition, or strife, or discord. May we put on the Lord Jesus Christ, and show our true faith by our godly and pious lives; may we let our light so shine before men that they may see our good works, and glorify our Father in heaven. And when our earthly days are numbered, O bring us to the blessed light of everlasting bliss, for the merits of Thy dear Son, our Saviour Jesus Christ. Amen.

Lassenius, 1686.

Tuesday Evening.

O THOU ever-present God, whose sacred presence fills the heavens and the earth, whither should we flee from Thy Spirit? Unto Thee do we lift up our eyes, O Thou who canst behold the innermost depths of our hearts; teach us now to pray to Thee with a real faith in Thy holy and gracious presence among us. O that we may now awaken from the sleep of security, that our immortal souls, now in the day of grace, may awaken unto true life! Have pity upon us, whom Thou hast called by Thy grace to walk in the way that leads to a blessed eternity. Ah! we confess before Thy all-seeing eyes, that we have not walked worthy of our high calling, nor of the great purposes for which Thou hast designed us. How many an hour has been spent in carelessness, in trivialities, or in actual departure from Thy ways! Yet Thou hast had compassion on us; Thou hast broken the snares that held us, and suffered us to experience Thy gracious help in Christ our Lord. May we never again do aught that shall make us lose Thy favour. Renew in us the sense of Thy gracious presence, and let it be a constant impulse within us to peace, trustfulness, and courage on our pilgrimage. Since Thou hast so mercifully inclined Thyself unto us, incline our hearts to Thee; let us see Thee with the eye of faith; let us hold Thee fast with a loving and adoring heart. O Lord, teach us to cling less and less, as life goes by, to this world with its thoughts and plans, and to turn away our eyes from its vanities. Let the remembrance that Thou art ever with us so fill our mind that we may be ever conversing with Thee, and never willing to forget Thee. We do not enough accustom ourselves to the thought of Thy presence; O make us more devout; let our affections be more fixed on Thee, that so the unbroken communion of our hearts with Thee may accompany us whatsoever we do, through life and in death. Teach us to pray heartily; to listen for Thy voice within, and never to stifle its warnings. Let us walk before Thee as becomes those who are priests unto God; give us grace to offer unto Thee gladly all that is ours, even what we love most dearly. Hast Thou not purchased, called, and chosen us to become Thy temple and Thy sanctuary? Behold, we bring our poor hearts as a sacrifice unto Thee: come and fill Thy sanctuary, and suffer nought impure to enter there. Guide and govern us; command us as Thou wilt, and let Thy laws be the sole rule of our conduct. O Thou who art Love, let Thy Divine Spirit flow like a river through our whole souls, and lead us in the right way till we pass by a peaceful death into the land of Promise. Amen.

Tersteegen, 1731.

Wednesday Morning.

COLLECT.

WE bless and praise and magnify Thee, O God of our fathers, who hast led us out of the shadows of night once more into the light of day. Unto Thy loving-kindness we make our entreaty; be merciful to our misdeeds; accept our prayers in the fullness of Thy compassions, for Thou art our refuge from one generation to another, O merciful and almighty God. Suffer the true Sun of Thy righteousness to shine in our hearts, enlighten our reason, and purify our senses; that so we may walk honestly as in the day, in the way of Thy commandments, and reach at last the life eternal, where we shall rejoice in Thy inaccessible light. For Thou art the Fountain of Life, and in Thy light shall we see light. Amen.

Greek Church.

PRAYER.

LORD, Thou hast searched us out and known us. Thou understandest all our ways. And Thou seest and knowest, O God, that we have a hearty desire so to live as Thou hast commanded Thy children, and according to the pattern that Jesus has left us. But, alas! how often we find that first one temptation, and then another, draws us aside from the right path. Sometimes we are seduced by our own hearts with their unchecked desires; sometimes enticed by the world with its evil examples; but in either case alike we displease Thee, and wound our own consciences. Therefore, we cry unto Thee to-day, O lead and guide us by Thy good Spirit in a plain path! Behold, we yield ourselves wholly unto Thee; as Thou didst lead Thy people through the sea and the desert into the Promised Land, so guide us through the dangers of life, and the wilderness and temptations of the world, with a good conscience and void of offence, till we reach the life eternal. Suffer us never henceforth willingly to sin against Thee, but to become in truth, and be known of all men to be, true and pious Christians. And if, in our weakness and folly, we even resist Thy Spirit, yet take Him not away, leave us not to our own will and guidance, for if we are left to ourselves we shall surely go astray. Give us a holy watchfulness in all we do and say, and write Thy love and fear in our hearts, that we may, in all that we do this day, govern ourselves by Thy word, and follow the example of our Blessed Lord, Jesus Christ. Amen.

Stark, 1740.

Wednesday Evening.

FATHER, with thankful and humble hearts we appear before Thee at the close of this day. We would thank Thee for all the benefits that we have received from Thy goodness. Under Thy care have we safely and calmly lived, preserved from many evils, kept in health and grace. Thou hast given us food and drink; Thou hast satisfied and refreshed us; with Thy help have we accomplished the duties of our family and our business, and it is to Thy blessing we owe what success we have found. Every fortunate circumstance we have met with; every opportunity for doing good; every impulse in the right way; the good we have done, and the evil we have been saved from doing; each victory we have gained over ourselves; the kindly comfort or wise counsel we have given or received; every sigh for the sufferings of others, and resolve to alleviate them; every thought of Thy presence, O Father; every silent but loving glance on the example of our Pattern, Thy Son our Lord—all are alike Thy gifts to us.

But, alas! how little, how imperfect is the good we have done; how much that might have been done have we left unattempted! We are the idle servants, who know their Lord's will, and yet do it but half or not at all. We confess that we come as sinners before Thee; yet it is to the mercy promised to us in Thy Son that we flee for refuge; Thy promise that Thou willest not the death of a sinner is our comfort. Teach us to know more truly how many and great are our faults, how deeply-seated the evil in our souls. Fain would we appear pure and unspotted before Thy holy eye; but who shall cleanse us from our impurities but Thyself? Speak to our souls the healing word: Be pure! Give us strength and wisdom to walk faithfully and joyfully in the way of willing obedience to Thy laws, and cheerful trust in Thy love. The best thanksgiving we can offer to Thee is to live according to Thy holy will; grant us every day to offer it more perfectly, and to grow in the knowledge of Thy will and the love thereof. Thou who art ever our Father and Saviour, be so especially in the darkness of night. Send us gentle sleep to refresh our bodies, that we may awaken to-morrow with renewed strength for Thy service. Avert all perils ; let no plague or terror come near our dwelling nor break our rest. Thou art my Father, I am Thy child—with this thought may each of us close his eyes to-night!

Father of all men! Guardian of all! yet ere we sleep let our intercessions for our fellow-men arise to Thee. Glorify Thyself and Thy goodness among all dwellers upon earth. Bless our friends and benefactors, our enemies and slanderers, if such there be. Protect the place where we dwell, and let all regions of the earth behold Thy mercy. Watch over this household and all whom we love far and near. Have pity on all sighing, weeping hearts who cannot find sleep. Grant us to sleep in peace and awake with cheerfulness, and may our first morning thought be to call Thee our Father, and to thank and praise Thee for Thy love. Amen.

Sailer, 1751–1832.

Thursday Morning.

O LORD, Almighty God, Father of Light, with whom is no change of darkness and light, from whom all good and perfect gifts do come, we pray unto Thee now for Thy great gift of faith. Increase in us from day to day by Thy Holy Spirit a true and lively faith in Thee and Thy Son Jesus Christ; that we may live worthily to Thy good pleasure, be fruitful in all good works, and grow in patience and forbearance, goodness and happiness. Give us strength according to the riches of Thy glory, that we may be strengthened with might in the inner man, and that Christ may dwell in our hearts by faith. O God, since no man knoweth the Son but the Father, and none can know the Father save the Son and he to whom the Son will reveal Him; draw us now, we pray Thee, to Thy Son, that He may lead us unto Thee. Give us to know Thy salvation, even the forgiveness of our sins. Since Thou hast kindled a spark of faith and trust in our hearts, and hast begun a good work within us, we pray Thee to perfect it unto the end, that we may become richer in all experience and wisdom, that we may be found pure and without offence in the day of the

Lord, filled with the fruits of righteousness to Thy glory. Preserve what Thou hast wrought in us, that we may show ourselves good soldiers of Christ, may keep our consciences blameless, and not suffer shipwreck in the time of trial and temptation. Suffer us not to be led astray by the many errors, divisions, and wrong opinions in the world. Guard us from superstition and all false worship, nor let us fall into doubt and unbelief. And give us Thy grace, that the faith Thou hast inspired be no dead inactive thing, but a living and mighty energy that shows itself in works of love, and shall bring us at last to the end of all faith, even the eternal blessedness of our souls; for Christ's sake. Amen.

Habermann, 1516-1590.

Thursday Evening.

O GOD our Lord, the stay of all them that put their trust in Thee, unto Thee we yield ourselves to-night. For he whose soul abideth in Thy grace and under Thy protection may walk in peace, untouched by any dread, for Thou holdest him in Thy right hand. Wherever Thou leadest we would go, for Thy ways are perfect wisdom and love. Even when we walk through the dark valley,

Thy light can shine into our hearts and guide us safely through the night of sorrow. Be Thou our Friend, and we need ask no more in heaven or earth; for Thou art the Comfort of all who trust in Thee, the Help and Defence of all who hope in Thee; the Rock on whom we would build; the strong Refuge wherein we may abide in safety. O Lord, we would be Thine; let us never fall away from Thee. We would accept all things without murmuring from Thy hand, for whatever Thou dost is right. If Thou sendest us darkness, yet Thou art good and we will praise Thee: if our path be brightness and peace, we praise Thee. Thy goodness ruleth over all things and at all times. Therefore we thank Thee, O heavenly Father, for all that Thy love and wisdom hath appointed unto us, for the bitter and the sweet of life, for joy and sorrow.

Only from one thing save us, we entreat Thee: let us not give way to sin and wickedness, nor rank ourselves among those who are not on Thy side. Blend our wills with Thine, and then we need fear no evil nor death itself, for all things must work together for our good. Lord, keep us in Thy love and truth; comfort us with Thy light; and guide us by Thy Holy Spirit. Amen.

Weiss, 1738-1805.

Friday Morning.

O LORD our God, we will praise Thee and speak of Thy love, for Thy goodness is unbounded, and Thy mercy is unfathomable. Great is Thy grace and glorious is Thy righteousness; long-suffering and faithful art Thou, and holy in all Thy works. Lord, we acknowledge our unworthiness and Thy greatness, our nothingness and Thy perfection. Without Thee we can do nothing, but Thou canst give us all things; we are weak, but in Thee is our strength; we are ignorant, but in Thee is our light; we are helpless, but Thou art the Fountain of all the good things that we enjoy. In truth, we are not worthy of the mercies that Thou hast bestowed on us. We praise Thee, O heavenly Father, that Thou hast created us in Thy image, and hast called on us to bring our souls and bodies a living sacrifice to Thee, which is our reasonable service. We therefore offer to Thee our wills; let us wish and purpose only what Thou wilt. We offer to Thee our lips; let us use them for Thy praise, not to utter shameful words or foolish and unseemly talk. We offer to Thee our members;

make them the instruments of righteousness, and let us not misuse them in any wrong or sinful act. We bring Thee our hearts, impure and blemished though they be; wash them in the blood of Christ, cleanse them by Thy Holy Spirit, sanctify them to be Thy temple wherein Thou reignest, filling them with living faith, grace and love. We consecrate to Thee our lives; may we live henceforward according to Thy Word, and obey in all things the inward voice of Thy Spirit.

So would we show our thankfulness to Thee; teach us to thank Thee better and better. Thou hast been our Guide from childhood, Thou hast led us wondrously, saved us in many a danger, preserved us from many a calamity. Thou hast comforted us in sorrow, and kept us from sinking under cares and anxieties. Thou hast heard our prayers, and borne with our misdoings. Therefore shall Thy praise be ever in our lips, now and for ever. Amen.

Modern, anon.

Friday Evening.

O GREAT and lofty God, Thou Father in the Highest, who hast promised to dwell with them that are of a lowly spirit and fear Thy Word; create now in us such lowly hearts, and give us a reverential awe of Thy commandments. What avails us this natural life, if we do not become partakers through the Spirit of Jesus Christ of Thy divine life? What will remain to us at the close of our temporal life, if we have not Thee, the true and eternal Life of our immortal souls? Lord, Thou knowest what distracted hearts we have, O give us self-recollection; Thou knowest what hard dead hearts we have, O touch and awaken us! Thou knowest how we yet resist Thy Word and our lower nature is reluctant to bow to Thy sceptre; therefore, O Lord, show forth Thy power, send Thy Spirit from on high to work among us, to make our hearts submissive, and ourselves capable of living in true union with Thee our Salvation, and of yielding implicitly to Thy grace.

O come, Thou Holy Spirit, and kindle our hearts with holy love; come, Thou Spirit of strength, and arouse our souls to hunger and thirst after Thee, their true Guide, that they may be sustained by Thy all-powerful influence. Arise, O Spirit of Life, that through Thee we may begin to live ; descend upon us and transform us into such human beings as the heart of God longs to see us, renewed into the image of Christ, and going on from glory to glory. O Spirit who searchest the deep things of God, suffer us to know by experience what we possess in our God and Saviour, that through this life-giving knowledge we may be made fervent in spirit, and strengthened to cleave to Him immovably. Work in us freedom from the bonds of earth and a pure love to each other ; bring about the establishment of Christ's kingdom within us, by imparting to us Thy righteousness, Thy peace, and Thy sacred gladness.

Come, Thou Stream of Eternity, who pourest in mighty flood from the throne of God, overflow our hearts, and sweep away all worldliness, leaving nought but what may live and grow hereafter in the Paradise of God.

Come and shed Thyself abroad in thousands of hearts which have been as yet without grace and love ; let children be born to Thee like the dew of the morning. Yea, let the dew of Thy grace descend abundantly on arid and lifeless souls, that many may be awakened, many born into the kingdom of heaven. O God, Thou Supreme Good, make Thyself known to us and glorify Thyself in our inner being. Have pity upon us, take not away Thy blessing from us for our unrighteousness ; do more than we are able to ask. Accompany us with Thy power, that we may bring forth rich fruits to the glory of Thy name. Hear us for Thine own sake, not for the sake of our poor prayers ; hear us for Jesus Christ's sake, and may He, our Mediator, unite His availing intercession with our weak sighs, and Thou, O Lord, seal it with an everlasting Yea and Amen.

Tersteegen, 1731.

Saturday Morning.

O MOST merciful God and Father, we commend ourselves and all that we have to Thine Almighty hands, and pray Thee to preserve us by Thy good Spirit from all sin, misfortune, and grief of heart. Give us the Spirit of grace and prayer, that we may have a consoling trust in Thy love, and that our sighs and petitions may be acceptable in Thy sight. Give us the Spirit of faith to kindle a bright flame of true and blessed faith in our hearts, that we may have a living knowledge of salvation, and our whole life may be a thank-offering for the mercies we have received. Give us the Spirit of love, that we may experience the sweetness of Thy love toward us, and also love Thee in return; and render our obedience not from constraint like slaves, but with the willing and joyful hearts of children. And let the love of Thee work in us a genuine love to our fellow-men, warm and unselfish, not considering what profit or harm we may expect from them, but ready always to do for them what we would have them do for us. Bless Thy word and all the means of grace to our use, and let us grow daily more and more,—

by patience, gentleness, sobriety, and humility, —into the likeness of Thy dear Son.

And we pray not only for ourselves, but according to His command for all men whom Thou hast created, redeemed, and called to Thy grace. Have mercy on the darkness in which so many nations and so large a portion of the world are yet lying, and let them be enlightened by the light of Thy dear Son and Thy holy Gospel. Have mercy on the whole Christian Church. Look especially on the congregations of faithful men to whom Thou hast entrusted the precious treasure of Thy true Gospel; preserve them in the faith, teach them to walk worthy of the high calling wherewith they are called; purify them from all abuses and evils, and let them bring forth much fruit. Have mercy on those congregations into which many errors have crept; lead them into the right way, and let all hearts be united in one Spirit in the bonds of love and peace, that at last divisions may have an end.

O bounteous God, pour out Thy blessing on all families, and on all the lawful occupations of men. Make our land fruitful, and suffer us to enjoy its fruits in health, peace, and thankfulness. Especially we commend to Thy fatherly goodness all who are in any affliction, the sick and the sorrowful, the tempted and the destitute, the captives and those who are oppressed by war or tyranny. Comfort them by Thy Holy Spirit; let not their trials be too sore for them; give them patience and an inward assurance of Thy goodness. Let their sufferings work together for the purifying of their souls and the renewal of the inner man; and in outward things do unto them as seemeth best to Thy fatherly wisdom. Now we commit ourselves and all Thy children everywhere into Thy hands; grant that in soul and body, in all our works and ways, we may show forth Thy glory and our gratitude, through Jesus Christ our only Saviour, to whom with Thee and the Holy Ghost be all praise and glory, for ever and ever. Amen.

Spener, 1676.

Saturday Evening.

COLLECT.

O LORD our God, who hast given peace to men, and hast sent down Thy Holy Spirit on Thy apostles and disciples, bestowing on them in Thy power fiery tongues wherewith to speak Thy praise; open also our lips, sinners though we be, and teach us to ask Thee aright for the right blessings. Steer Thou the vessel of our life toward Thyself, Thou tranquil Haven of all storm-tost souls. Show us the course wherein we should go. Renew a willing spirit within us. Let Thy Spirit curb our wayward senses, and guide and ennoble us unto that which is our true good, to keep Thy laws, and in all our works evermore to rejoice in Thy glorious and gladdening Presence. Let us not be deluded by the fleeting pleasures of this world, but strengthen us that we may aspire to the enjoyment of that which is to come. For Thine is the glory and praise from all Thy saints for ever and ever. Amen.

Basil, ✠ 379.

PRAYER.

O GRACIOUS and merciful God, we come before Thy face to-day with thanks and praise, that through the past week Thou hast so mercifully preserved us, and so richly blessed the labour of our hands. Thou hast watched over our goings-out and comings-in, and hast been around our path and blessed us both in body and soul. Therefore we thank Thee from the bottom of our hearts.

And now we would depart from earthly business and daily cares, and build a temple, a house of prayer in our hearts, wherein to worship God alone. O! how great is His kindness in having appointed unto men a day of rest from their toil. This rest is an image of the heavenly rest which is to come,—the perfect rest that remaineth for the children of God in the life eternal, when they shall be freed from toil and pain, from sorrow and sin. O gracious God, may we spend the Sunday before us in Thy fear and grace. Give us Thy Holy Spirit, that we may consecrate the whole day to Thee and Thy service. Early shall our prayers arise to Thee; to Thee will we sing and pray in the great congregation. Keep alive the devotion of our hearts; and let no earthly cares creep in to draw them away. When Thy Word is preached, open our hearts to receive it as a precious treasure; may it purify, convert, and change them, that we may grow not only in years, but in faith and piety, and become new creatures and living members of the body whereof Christ our Lord is the Head. So let us spend one Sabbath after another, until Thou bring us to the eternal Sabbath of heavenly joy, through Jesus Christ our only Redeemer and Saviour. Amen.

Stark, 1740.

SECOND WEEK.

Sunday Morning.

COLLECT.

O HEAVENLY Father, awaken Thou our devotion, that on this and every Sunday, we may keep the sacred day of rest according to Thy will. Grant us grace to rest from all sinful deeds and thoughts, to surrender ourselves wholly unto Thee, and to keep our souls still before Thee like a still lake; that so the beams of Thy grace may be mirrored therein, and may kindle in our hearts the glow of faith and love and prayer. May we, through such stillness and hope, find strength and gladness in Thee, O God, now and evermore. Amen.

Embden, 1595-1650.

PRAYER.

OUR Father in heaven and earth, we thank Thee in the Name of our Lord Jesus Christ, that Thou hast guarded us from all the perils of the past night, and brought us, through Thy undeserved goodness, safe and well to this blessed day. O Thou whose love never faileth, let the memory of our past sins vanish from before Thy countenance like the darkness of the night that is fled. Awaken our hearts from the slumber of idleness and folly, and let us arise with Christ from the death of sin to a new life of righteousness. O Father of lights and Giver of all good and perfect gifts, give us to-day Thy gracious Word, and may it be the highest joy and delight of our hearts. May it be a Word of truth spoken according to Thy will, and may we receiving it be born again of the Spirit, and become the first-fruits of Thy creatures. Pour upon us, therefore, richly the grace of Thy Holy Spirit, that both at home and in Thy house we may be quick to listen to, and careful to heed Thy precious Word ; but slow to all vain and empty talk, which cannot profit us but only grieves Thy Spirit in our hearts. O Almighty Father, give us seeing eyes, hearing ears, and understanding hearts that we may be aware of our own wants, and gladly gather whatever Thy hand to-day may let fall for us. Plant Thy Word within us, and let it make this day a happy one. And to all who shall to-day preach Thy holy Name, whether in this place or elsewhere, throughout all Christendom, give Thy Spirit, that they may truly proclaim Thy Word and not their own.

Yes, come with Thy dear Son in one Spirit to us, and keep Thy Sabbath-day of rest in our souls. Let our hearts be Thy temple, wherein Thy Spirit unites us in true faith to Christ, and leads us in true love unto thankful obedience to Thee; so shall we be enabled to offer Thee perpetually an acceptable worship. Lead us on from faith to faith, from love to love, from strength to strength, until we reach the end of our pilgrimage, and are made meet for that world, where we shall keep the eternal Sabbath of unbroken rest, with all the people of God and His holy angels, in the secure mansions of peace. So shall we ever thank and love and praise Thee for all Thy love and Thy great goodness, through Jesus Christ our Lord. Amen.

G. Arnold, 1697.

Sunday Evening.

PRAYER.

O THOU gracious and merciful God, Thou Lover of Mankind, we thank Thee with our whole hearts for the vast unspeakable love wherewith Thou, O God and Father of souls, hast loved us. Thou dost bear us on Thy heart ; Thou dost never forget nor forsake us ; Thou carest for us ; Thou hearest our prayers ; Thou countest all our tears and sighs, Thou knowest all our sorrows ; Thine eye pierceth the depth of our hearts ; Thy inner voice revealeth to us Thy precious promises of grace and help, of consolation and forgiveness, of eternal life.

Thou hast given to us Thy dear Son : and in sending Him to take our flesh upon Him, Thou hast assured us of Thy goodness and Thy readiness to aid. By His Gospel dost Thou teach and comfort us ; in His earthly walk and conversation hast Thou shown us the Pattern and the Way to a holy life ; His life and death have redeemed us from eternal death ; His resurrection has plucked the sting from the grave ; His ascension has opened the way to Heaven, where He hath prepared a place for us. Thou hast quickened and strengthened us by Thy Holy Spirit, and given us in Him the witness that we are children of God and heirs of an eternal inheritance. Yea, Thou hast bestowed on us not only countless benefits, but even Thyself, O God, with Thy beloved Son and the Holy Spirit. O how can we thank Thee sufficiently for Thy great goodness ! Thy love is eternal and never ceases: it is infinitely higher than the heavens, broader than the earth, deeper than the abyss, wider than from sunrise to sunset. As high as the heavens above the earth, so great is Thy mercy toward them that fear Thee; as far as the east is from the west, so far hast Thou put our trangressions from Thee; for Thou pitiest us, even as a father pitieth his children.

Lord, give us hearts never to forget Thy love; but to dwell therein whatever we do, whether we walk or sit, sleep or wake, live or die, or rise again to the life that is to come. For Thy love is eternal life and everlasting rest; for this is life eternal to know Thee and Thy infinite goodness. O let its flame never be quenched in our hearts; let it grow and brighten, till our whole souls are glowing and shining with its light and warmth. Turn away our hearts from all idols; be Thou our Joy and Hope, our Strength and Life, our Shield and Shepherd, our Portion for ever. For happy are we if we continue in the love wherewith Thou hast loved us; holy are we when we love Thee steadfastly. But wretched and miserable are we when we fall away from Thee, for then we lose the only true good, we fall out of light into darkness, out of life into death. Therefore O Thou, whose name and essence is love, enkindle our hearts, enlighten our understandings, sanctify our will, cleanse and fill all the thoughts of our hearts, for Jesus Christ's sake. Amen.

J. Arndt, 1555–1621.

Monday Morning.

THE night is departed; the daylight is come; awake then, O soul and heart, praise our God, and meditate on what His will appointeth unto thee to-day to do for Him!

O Lord God, Father, Son, and Holy Spirit, Thou art the only true and living God, who hast made heaven and earth, light and darkness, day and night, times and seasons, and hast maintained them in unshaken order for the welfare of us Thy children. Thou hast been our Guardian through this night, and that we are yet united together, that we are alive and well, is of Thy goodness. We thank Thee that Thou hast kept us in the shelter of Thy hand, so that when darkness was around us, when sleep had closed our eyes, and we lay helpless and lonely in unconsciousness, Thou hast guarded us from sin and shame, from fear and terror, from harm and loss, from sickness and death. And we would remember in this morning hour the many benefits we have received from Thy fatherly hand; how Thou didst create us with soul and body, when as yet we were not; didst redeem us when we were lost; didst sanctify us when we had forsaken Thee; and hast preserved us to this day, though we are not worthy of Thy care. And since we receive all these Thy gifts afresh with the new day, and are as it were born afresh to a new life, so let us anew offer ourselves unto Thee, and praise and love and honour Thee with all we are and all we have, to-day and for evermore.

Now, O my God, Thou knowest that every day hath also its own trouble; that we are sinful and weak and heavy-laden, and every morning feel anew our cares and our infirmities. Let not then Thy kindness cease from us, visit us not for our sins with Thy displeasure; forsake us not, that the enemy of our souls may have no advantage over us. Let not to-day be a day of falling in which we trifle with Thy grace; let not our conscience sleep, O Father of Light, when our bodily eyes are open; let us do and say and think and undertake nothing that can hurt our neighbour or our own souls. May we put on the Lord Jesus Christ and His righteousness, and as children of light be found of Thee and all men, God-fearing, just, truthful, upright, prudent, modest, and temperate. Let us not eat the bread of idleness; but let all indolence, indifference, and disorder be far from our occupations. Let us throughout the day fulfil the necessary duties of our various callings, forgetting nothing, neglecting nothing; failing neither through haste and impatience, nor a presumptuous procrastination. O Lord, we will do all things to-day in Thy name, so let us begin with gladness and end with joy. Show us Thyself in everything how we may best promote Thy glory and be of use to others. Grant us to bear the burden and heat of the day with patience, and give us to-day our daily bread. To Thee we commit ourselves from morn to evening; prosper Thou our words and works.

Gracious God and merciful Father! Thou hast once more caused Thy sun to rise on the evil and the good. Have mercy then on both; and let no human being this day fall to utter ruin whether of body or soul. Grant that to-day throughout Christendom Thou mayst be truly served; that in all temporal government some good and wise measures may be resolved on; that in every family something useful may be accomplished; and so this day may be hallowed by each in his own way and to Thy glory. Hear Thou Thy pious children who cry to Thee in the morning. Forgive the godless who are beginning the day without prayer, and are about to spend one more day without Thee. Look down in pity on all the sick and suffering, the sorrowful, and the timid. Be the guide of the travellers who are starting to-day upon their journey. Provide for the poor who know not this day what they may have to eat and drink. Grant to all who would gain an honest living the opportunity of work to-day; and let all labourers fulfil with honesty their daily task. Guard those whose lawful work summons them to danger; and uphold those who sink and are weary beneath the burden of their toil. To Thee we commend ourselves, those whom we love, all with whom we come in contact; have mercy, O God, on all Thy creatures, and Thine be the praise and the glory for ever and ever. Amen.

Neumann, 1648–1715.

Monday Evening.

COLLECT.

LORD God, who dwellest in the light that no man can approach unto, Thou hast guided us by Thy great mercy throughout this day. Accept now the prayers of us Thy unworthy servants; save us from the darkness of sin, and so enlighten the eyes of our soul that we, walking in Thy light and continuing in Thy fear, may behold Thy wonders, and evermore praise Thee, the only true and gracious God. For Thine is the kingdom and the power and the glory. Amen.

Greek Church.

PRAYER.

O LORD Jesu Christ, our Saviour, and the Source of all blessings, now that the sun with its light hath departed, its place is filled with myriads of bright and lovely stars, which preach to us anew of Thy unspeakable goodness. For the heavens do tell the glory of God and the firmament showeth His handiwork. Let us then as Thy rational creatures join our voices to their hymn of praise, and thank and bless Thee for the goodness which has been our guide, our defence, and our happiness throughout this day. We own that our manifold sins and transgressions have justly merited Thy displeasure, yet of Thy great mercy Thou dost grant us forgiveness, and dost bestow on us the night with its peaceful rest and quiet sleep. We now lay our bodies down to slumber, and lay our souls, O Lord, at Thy precious feet. Let Thy power and grace preserve them through the hours of darkness. If

be not we that live, but Christ in us; and that, by faith in the Son of God, we may grow and blossom in righteousness to Thy praise, and bring forth the fruits of good living to the profit and service of all with whom we have to do. Once more we surrender ourselves to Thee, O Father. Do with us even as Thou wilt; purify and uphold us that we may live as Christian men ought to do, and as members of the Israel of God, with whom is mercy and peace. We ask no honour but to be Thy children, no riches but the righteousness of Christ, no joy but that which springs from the indwelling of Thy Holy Spirit.

Thou wilt provide for our temporal wants, for Thou hast said, "I will never leave thee nor forsake thee;" yet guard us from idleness; and let us labour not for mere hope of gain, but in sincere desire to be of use in our generation. Let Thy mercy be extended unto all the dwellers upon earth, and Thy goodness be over all Thy creatures. Remember for good Thy children who know Thee, and are bound together in the unity of the Spirit to own one glorious Head Jesus Christ. Let the prayers of each arise as one prayer before Thee, through Christ in whom Thou hast accepted us. Be Thou the eternal reward of those who have shown kindness to us; and look on our enemies with a pitying eye, and forgive them, as we forgive them from our hearts. We commend all who are dear to us to Thy loving arms. We commit to Thee all churches and schools, all who rule, and all who serve. O God, behold how much sadness and sin there is in all classes; arise and help us to put an end to ungodliness and sin, that Thy glory may be made known. Help all the poor and sorrowful who cry to Thee; and despise not these our imperfect prayers, but hear us for the sake of Jesus Christ our Lord. Amen.

A. H. Franke, 1663–1727.

Tuesday Evening.

COLLECT.

O THOU, our Lord and our God, our merciful Father in Heaven, we entreat Thee with childlike hearts, give us in this world whatever is really good and happy for us in soul and body, according to Thy holy will and pleasure. May we believe truly in Thy holy Word, live as Christians, endure with patience, and at last die in peace and hope, for Jesus Christ's sake. Amen.

Quirsfeld, 1641-1686.

PRAYER.

O THOU, our God, how great and glorious, how rich and mighty, art Thou! All things belong to Thee, and Thou canst bestow them as Thou wilt. Behold, we come to Thee and ask for Thy gifts. We have nothing of our own but sin; for whatever of good there is in us or around us comes from Thee alone, from whom all perfect gifts proceed.

O Father, make us rich in Thy spiritual blessings. Give us Thy Holy Spirit; give us loving and pious hearts; help us to strive to control our desires, to lay aside evil habits, to keep ourselves unspotted from the world, and to yield ourselves in soul and body a living sacrifice to Thee, which is our reasonable service. Behold, O God, to how many dangers and temptations we are subject in this world; guide us by Thy power, that we may not be led astray to depart from Thee. Abide Thou in our souls, rule our hearts, and vouchsafe unto us grace to become new creatures, living members in the Body of Christ; then shall we have enough of riches, honour, and gladness for this world.

Yet also, O gracious Father, give us whatever earthly blessings are good for us: Thou seest all our needs, Thou knowest what we want; yet give not according to our will, but Thine. If health be good for us, give us such bodily strength as may enable us to fulfil our appointed tasks rightly and happily. Accompany us in all our ways, guard us from misfortune; bless our undertakings, for it is of Thy blessing that true success cometh. Thou hast placed us in this world, and Thou knowest how to feed and provide for us here. On Thee we cast our cares, care Thou for Thy children; preserve and protect them; let us richly enjoy Thy fatherly and faithful providence.

O God, hear the voice of our prayer, and refuse not the request of our lips. Bestow on us in earthly things whatever is wholesome for us and pleasing to Thee; but in heavenly things pour upon us a bountiful measure of Thy grace. Be with us to our life's end, and then bring us as Thy children to the assembly of the saints in light; so let us here be united to Thee in faith and love, and there in the blessed vision of Thy glory for ever and ever. For Jesus Christ's sake. Amen.

Reiz, 1750.

Wednesday Morning.

COLLECT.

BLESSED Lord, grant unto us Thy Holy Spirit to work in us daily a true and lasting repentance, and keep us ever as contrite Christian people willing to acknowledge, bewail, and lament our sins; yet also keep us ever, O Lord, steadfast and strong in our faith in the forgiveness of sins, and in our purpose to amend our lives, through Jesus Christ our Lord. Amen.

Eichhorn, 1546.

PRAYER.

O LORD our God, holy and incomprehensible, who hast commanded the light to shine out of darkness; who hast refreshed us by nightly slumbers, and hast awakened us again to praise Thy name and call upon Thy grace; accept in Thy endless compassion our morning sacrifice of worship and thanksgiving, and grant unto us all such requests as may be wholesome for us. Make us, O Lord, children of the light and of the day, and heirs of Thy eternal inheritance. In the multitude of Thy mercies, remember, O Lord, for good Thy whole people; all who with us pray to Thee, all our brethren by land or sea, or wherever else they may be, in Thy vast kingdom, who need Thy grace and help; and pour upon us all the riches of Thy goodness. That so, redeemed in body and soul, and unwavering in faith and trust, we may bless Thy holy and wonderful name evermore. Amen.

Greek Church.

Wednesday Evening.

O LORD, Thou eternal God, with whom is no change of light and darkness, for Thou abidest the same for ever, and Thy years have no end; day and night are Thine, and it is Thou who keepest the sun and the stars in their appointed courses. Thou helpest us to pass through each day as it comes, to lay down each burden in turn, and it is through Thy goodness we have now reached this present night. If in this past day we have grown not older only, but better, wiser, healthier, or happier, we owe it all to Thee. Therefore we thank Thee now at evening-tide for all the blessings of the day; that Thou hast given us not only the day for labour, but the night for repose; that Thou hast heard our morning prayer, and hast showered on us many enjoyments through the day; that Thou hast preserved our lives and health, fed us and cared for us, governed our thoughts and enlightened our eyes. For it is through Thy guidance that we have prospered to-day in our undertakings, and our works have been accomplished, so that we may now lie down to sleep in peace, with cheerful and thankful hearts. Once more have we cause to exclaim 'How precious are Thy thoughts unto me, O God; Thy thoughts are very deep.' And if some evil have befallen us to-day, if all has not happened according to our wishes, yet we confess we have deserved far worse at Thy hands, and should have been far more miserable but for the alleviations of Thy mercy.

But, O gracious and long-suffering God, though Thou hast cared for us to-day, we have often forgotten Thee. Thou hast given us much for which we never prayed; we have sinned, and Thou hast still had patience with us. O blessed Father, we thank and praise Thee for this kindness, for all the mercies Thou hast poured to-day on us and on all men, and the love that has averted so much evil from us all. Forgive us, for Thy dear Son Jesus Christ's sake, for all the evil we have done or the good we have omitted to do, whether towards Thee or our neighbour or ourselves. Yea, do Thou in mercy efface and make up for any injury that we may have done by our faults to others or to our own souls. Keep us this night from all works of darkness, and whether we wake or sleep, let our thoughts and deeds be in accordance with Thy holy will. Preserve us from all dangers and terrors of the night; from restless watching and sorrowful thoughts; from unnecessary or fretful cares and imaginary fears; from sickness, and from violent or painful death. Let us awake to-morrow renewed in strength, and cheerful in spirits; may we arise with holy thoughts, and go forth to live to Thine honour, to the service of our fellow-men, and the comfort and joy of our own households. Hear us, O Lord, for Christ's sake. Amen.

Neumann, 1690.

Thursday Morning.

COLLECT.

WITH the morning doth our heart awaken unto Thee, O God, for Thy commandments are our light upon earth. Teach us to follow after justice and holiness in Thy fear; for Thou art our glory, the only true God. Incline Thine ear unto us, O Lord, who are here met to call upon Thy name together; save us by Thy mighty hand, bless Thy people and sanctify Thy inheritance; give peace to Thy world, to Thy Church and Thy people. And Thine be the glory now and for evermore throughout eternity. Amen.

Greek Church.

PRAYER.

O MERCIFUL God, whose loving-kindness and faithfulness are new every morning, we once more thank Thee with heart and lips that Thou hast bade us arise from our beds in health and peace, and hast preserved our bodies from harm and our souls from sin. How great is Thy goodness, O Lord, so that men trust under the shadow of Thy wings, and find there a secure refuge.

Once more we behold the daylight, give us therefore grace to walk in the light, and avoid the works of darkness. May we count that day as lost wherein we have bowed to the service of the evil world, and ruled our lives by its fashions and follies, of which we shall have to give account at Thy judgment-seat. Let us rather consecrate ourselves to Thy service; in all our wishes, thoughts, and undertakings may we seek what is pleasing in Thy sight, and may the whole day thus be hallowed to Thee. Let us ever so live and speak and act as though this day might be our last.

But now, O Lord, after the dark hours wherein we lay as children in Thy fatherly arms, Thou hast once more bestowed, as it were, a new life upon us, whither then shall we turn but to Thee? We knock at Thy door of grace, we approach the Fountain of blessing, whence mercy after mercy, help after help, is ever flowing forth to the children of men. Give us counsel when we are in perplexity, direct and control all our plans by Thy will; kindle in us such a flame of love, that we may to-day show our Christian faith in our works, and continue in charity with Thee and our neighbours, till we reach the evening in the peace of a good conscience. What Thou

sick; guard our little ones; shorten the hours of darkness by Thy presence, to those who cannot sleep, to all sufferers in mind or body who are looking forward to them with dread. Finally, be Thou the Guardian of our whole community from peril and loss, and whether this night be like all the past ones to us, or to anyone of us be the last, may we alike be found safe in Thy gracious keeping. So bring us all in Thine own time from this world of darkness to Thine eternal light and peace and rest; for Jesus Christ's sake. Amen.

M. Ritter, 1689.

Friday Morning.

CREATE in us, O God, a pure heart, and put a new spirit within us; cast us not away from the light of Thy countenance, and take not Thy Holy Spirit from us. Comfort us, O Lord, with Thy continual aid, and let Thy joyful Spirit preserve our steps. Let us now begin with our whole hearts, to lead a new life that shall be pleasing in Thy sight. Inspire us with a firm and steadfast resolution to grow holier and better with every day, that so our piety may be no hypocrisy, but a genuine reality, and we may not serve Thee with false or divided hearts. Let us not follow and imitate the world, as we have done, but show us what is that good and perfect will of God, that our minds may be bent to fulfil it. May there be no deceitfulness in our love to Thee or to our neighbours. Let us hate that which is evil, and cleave to that which is good; let brotherly love towards all our fellow-creatures so glow in our hearts, that we may ever meet them with kindness and with respect. May we not be slothful in business, but fervent in spirit, joyful in hope, patient in trial, persevering in prayer. Teach us, O Lord, to care for the necessities of our fellow-Christians, to rejoice with them that do rejoice, and to weep with them that weep. So let us continually grow in all points more like to Christ who is our Head, that we may seek no more the pleasures of the world, but live to the will of God. For the past time of our lives is enough to have spent in carelessness; henceforward may we walk as children of light, and have no fellowship with the unfruitful works of darkness. May we add to our faith, virtue; and to virtue, modesty; and to modesty, temperance; and to temperance, patience; and to patience, brotherly love; and to brotherly love, the love of all mankind. For if Thou grant us, through Thy help, that these virtues dwell in us richly, they will not suffer us to be idle or unfruitful in the service of our Lord and Master, Jesus Christ. Grant this, O merciful Father, for the love of Thy only Son, and through the power of Thy Holy Spirit. Amen.

Quirsfeld, 1642–1686.

Friday Evening.

SPIRIT of the Almighty, who descendest upon us to consecrate us as a temple of God; O let us now experience what strength and consolation lie in the knowledge that Thy life-giving Breath is breathing yet among us. We open to Thee our breasts; we yield to Thee our hearts; grant us to feel the peace which Thou alone canst bestow.

Accomplish Thy perfect work in our souls; let us become day by day purer, freer, more heavenly, more happy, and preserve us unto eternal life. Bless, animate, and sustain us, and raise us mightily above all that would distract us, to Thyself and the consciousness of Thy fellowship which gives joy to all who dwell therein. As yet we are bound with many chains; we tarry among things seen and temporal, and feel their oppression; we are exposed to the storms of the outer world, and are wrestling with its ills. But we are not dismayed, for we are more than earth and dust, we are akin to Thee, O Spirit of the Lord, and can experience Thy heavenly influence. Thou bearest witness with our spirits that we are the children of God; O, for the sake of the Father' love who has given us His only Son, of the Son's compassion who has shed His blood for us, help our weakness ; and when we know not how to pray aright, plead Thou for us with sighs that cannot be uttered. Scatter the delusions which so often hide Truth from our eyes ; help us to control the inclinations which so oft rebel against Thy holy Law ; teach us to recognise ever more clearly and vividly that he only is wise who obeys Thee, he only is happy who follows Thy impulses. Every moment that we spend here is so important! And yet there are so many dangers ; and yet we forget so easily how swiftly the time of preparation is passing away! O make us wise in time; quicken our faith in the better world that awaits us, and give us strength to begin to live for it here and now. Unite us ever more closely to the company of faithful hearts whom Thou art sanctifying and preparing for heaven ; fill us with their faith and love and hope. For it is from Thee, the Spirit of the Lord, whose mighty working fills the holy temple of Christ's Church on earth, that we expect all good things. Perfect, then, the good work which Thou hast begun in us, and seal us unto the day of Jesus Christ. Amen.

Reinhard, 1753-1813.

Saturday Morning.

O ALMIGHTY God and Heavenly Father, who wast from the beginning and dost endure for ever: we worship Thee, we glorify Thee, we praise Thee, we thank Thee with our whole hearts, for all the manifold benefits Thou hast bestowed upon us. We thank Thee that Thou hast created by Thy Almighty Power and Divine Word the heavens and the earth, the sun and moon, and all the creatures which Thy wisdom governs and preserves. O Lord, how glorious are Thy works: they exist through Thy power, and serve Thee according to the purpose which Thou hast imparted to them. The sun arises and proclaims the day, and tells us the wondrous work of the Most High; the shining stars adorn the heaven, and Thy Word holds them in their courses. We thank Thee, O God, for the creatures of this lower earth, and that Thou hast made it and them so serviceable and precious to our race. But, above all, we thank Thee, O our Maker, that Thou hast made us rational human beings, created in Thine own image, gifted with soul and body, with the reason and senses Thou dost bestow and preserve. How can we tell all thy wonders, or speak all Thy praises? We who have transgressed against Thee, can never declare aright how much we owe Thee, nor offer Thee a worthy tribute of thanksgiving. But, Lord, let us not therefore keep silence; help us never to forget all the manifold goodness Thou hast shown us; may we ever remember and talk of Thy righteousness, Thy mercy and grace; may our lips be full of Thy praises, and may we say, 'I will give thanks unto the Lord in His sanctuary; I will praise Him in the strength of His power and in His mighty deeds; I will speak of His great glory; let all things that have life and breath give thanks to our Lord.' Amen.

Habermann, 1516–1590.

Saturday Evening.

O GRACIOUS and merciful God, we thank Thee that Thou hast suffered us to reach the close of this week in peace, and hast not summoned us away amid our transgressions. For we confess that we have done much that is evil, and left undone much good that we might have done; that we have served neither Thee nor our fellow-men as we ought. O Father, we have sinned and done evil in Thy sight; yea, and we see both the wickedness and the punishment of sin, and yet we cannot escape from it. We are grieved and sorrowful for it; we should despair of ourselves and our own powers, but we have one refuge: we surrender ourselves wholly unto Thee, and implore Thee to accept us according to Thy promise, and to quicken us anew with the strength and comfort of Thy Spirit.

O Lord, we know that Thou dost invite the weary to come unto Thee, dost save them that are ready to perish, and enfold with Thy grace the helpless and the comfortless. Strengthen then our faith to lay a firm hold upon the promises of Thy gracious covenant; let us realise within ourselves its endless blessings, its eternal righteousness and glory, redemption and blessedness; grant us to know that they are ours; yet O grant us never to misuse or reap hurt from these or any other of Thy good gifts. O Holy Spirit, awaken within us a hearty desire for the day of the Lord, that we may use it aright in prayer and devotion, and find the true rest and joy of our souls in the hearing of Thy Word and the many spiritual blessings Thou dost so richly bestow on us.

Show us the beauty of Thy sanctuary; let us hear the sweet voice of our great Shepherd; prepare our hearts by faith, humility, and love to receive our Lord, and to find gladness and satisfaction in His presence. So may the coming Sabbath be a day of holy delight to us, and may we begin and end it to Thy glory, and the profit and progress of our own souls in all goodness. For Jesus Christ's sake. Amen.

Riga Prayer Book, 1707.

THIRD WEEK.

Sunday Morning.

PRAYER.

O THOU holy and infinite God, our Father in Christ Thy only begotten Son, we come before Thy Face and desire to worship Thee ; stir up our hearts to do so by Thy Holy Spirit.

We bless Thee, we thank Thee, O Lord, for the free mercy and grace wherewith Thou hast hitherto borne with us, for all the unspeakable love and truth which Thou hast shown us in Thy fatherly compassion. Oh, how slothful and lukewarm, how negligent have we been in responding to Thy goodness ! How little impression have Thy grace, Thy Spirit, and Thy love made on our hearts ! Alas ! we were so far from Thee that we gave no heed to the tokens of Thy kindness ; but now we humble ourselves before Thee ; grant that we may do so in sincerity, and have our hearts bowed down with true penitence.

And then, O Lord, renew us; let Thy Spirit shed abroad the first love in our hearts. O let Thy love so inflame us that we may gladly surrender ourselves with all we are and have unto Thee and loving Thee, our God, may renounce the world and all that is in it, and cleave to Thee alone. O Jesus, who didst inspire Thy first disciples with such an ardour of love that they joyfully risked all earthly good and life itself for Thy sake, let Thy love fall as fire from heaven upon the altar of our hearts; teach us to guard it heedfully by continual devotion and quietness of mind, and to cherish with anxious care every spark of its holy flame with which Thy good Spirit would quicken us, so that neither height, nor depth, things present nor things to come, may ever separate us therefrom. O have pity on our souls which are hastening towards eternity! How little are we ready, how dimly burn our lamps! How little are we prepared to renounce all that is of the earth alone, and desire with true fervour Thyself and Thy salvation! Strengthen Thou our souls; awaken us from the deathly sleep which holds us captive; animate our cold hearts with Thy warmth and tenderness, that we may no more live as in a dream, but walk before Thee as pilgrims in earnest to reach their home. And grant us all at last to meet with Thy holy saints before Thy throne, and there rejoice in Thy love for ever and ever. Amen.

Tersteegen, 1731.

Sunday Evening.

PRAYER.

O LORD, our God and Father, how shall we thank Thee for Thy love which has led us out of the darkness of error, and for Thy grace which would fain raise us unhappy slaves to sin, into Thy eternal freedom and blessedness? Ah, what were we without Thy Word and the comfort of Thy promises? Lord, how can we magnify Thy name enough, how can we make our whole lives show forth the praise of Thy righteousness?

Father, Thou knowest that alone we can do nothing. Behold, we seek Thee, but of ourselves we cannot find Thee; we long for Thy light, but we cannot illuminate our own souls; we desire Thy grace, but alone we cannot win it; we know Thy will, but without Thy support we are unable to fulfil it. Help us, therefore, since we cannot help ourselves; send down Thy Spirit into our hearts that whatever we are or do it may be to Thy glory ; may He purify, enlighten, strengthen, and sanctify us !

Let not Thy Word have been spoken in vain to us, and grant that we may be not hearers only, but doers of the same, and that it may bring forth the true fruits of salvation in our hearts. Turn not Thy Face from us, and withdraw not Thy grace ; lead us ever in the right way, and let Thy Holy Spirit encourage us ; may we never sink back into darkness, nor into error, but let the light of Thy life shine on us evermore. Teach us to do according to Thy pleasure, and take not away Thy good Spirit from us. Amen.

Weiss, 1738-1805.

Monday Morning.

COLLECT.

LORD Jesu Christ, our Strength, our Rock, our Fortress, our Deliverer, our God and Lord in whom we trust ; we thank and praise Thee from our hearts, that Thou hast bidden us awake from sleep in health and comfort. Awaken also our inmost hearts and souls, that to-day and throughout the coming week we may serve Thee obediently, and faithfully perform the duties of our several callings ; and awaken us at last one day with joy to the life eternal. Amen.

Stölzlein, 1603-1677.

PRAYER.

O LORD, heavenly Father, eternal God, we praise Thee for Thy goodness and the wondrous works that Thou doest for the children of men. Never will we forget Thy kindness ; accept then the sacrifice of thanksgiving which we bring to Thee in this morning hour. We cry unto Thee to keep us this day from all dangers to body and soul ; and give command to Thy holy angels to watch over us in all our ways. Lead us in the way of Thy commandments, that we may walk blameless in Thy service as the children of the day whom Thou lovest. Guard us from the enemy of our souls and the occasions of sin in the world ; guard us from our own weakness and evil desires, that we be not overpowered by them to act against Thee, and to kindle Thy anger with our sins. Rule us by Thy Holy Spirit, that we may undertake, speak and think nothing but what is pleasing to Thee and tends to the honour of Thy divine majesty.

Behold, O God, we yield ourselves wholly, both inwardly and outwardly, in soul and body, with all our powers and energies, to Thy will. Accept us as a living sacrifice holy and acceptable in Thy sight, that so we may render to Thee our reasonable service. O Almighty Father, make us Thine own, govern every thought and affection, that we may care to know nothing beyond Thee. Lord, early shall our voice ascend to Thee ; be Thou attentive to our prayer ; early will we praise Thee, and in the evening we will not cease to speak unto Thee, through Jesus Christ. Amen.

Habermann, 1516–1590.

Monday Evening.

ALMIGHTY and everlasting God, we confess and lament before Thee that we have not been so faithful and diligent in our various occupations to-day as we ought to have been; too often are we slothful and negligent, not fervent in spirit, serving the Lord. But Thou, who art the Fountain of all true blessing and success, Thou who willest that we Thy fallen creatures should be delivered from the curse of sin, and brought to the blessing of Thy love in Christ Jesus—give us now wisdom and understanding, that henceforward we may work in accordance with Thy will, to the glory of Thy Name, and the profit of our neighbours and ourselves. And since our own evil nature is the greatest hindrance to Thy blessing, do Thou preserve us from all misuse of Thy gifts. Let them not seduce us to pride, covetousness, or self-indulgence; let us take no credit for them to ourselves, but ascribe them solely to Thee, the Giver of all good things. Control our self-will, which is ever impatient to escape from Thy guidance; that so Thy will only be done in and through us, and we may follow the example of our Saviour when He was living on this earth. Shed abroad His gentleness and humility in our hearts, that we may abide like Him in love to all men ; and that Thou mayest work by us as instruments in Thy hand, even as Thou wilt to Thy honour. Unite our hearts so closely to Thee that Thou mayest be able to use us for Thy gracious purposes in whatever way Thou seest to be right and beneficial. Unto Thee would we yield ourselves and all that Thou hast given us. We renounce our self-love and self-will, for therein is our greatest torment, and cast ourselves on the power of Thy love and Thy blessing, wherein is our peace. Pour down, then, Thy blessing on our work, and when at last this toilsome life is ended, grant us to enter into eternal rest and joy, through Jesus Christ our faithful Saviour. Amen.

Gerhardt and Arnold.

Tuesday Morning.

O BLESSED Father, we come to Thee and pray for that Spirit which Thou hast graciously promised to bestow on all them that call upon Thee. Send Him down from Thy holy dwelling into our hearts, that He may be our Guide and lead us according to Thy law to perform what is well pleasing in Thy sight.

Alas! we see so many misleading paths in life, so many around us who walk in them, that we cry, Lead us into Thy truth, unite our hearts to fear Thy Name; set before our eyes how surely the broad way ends in destruction. Bestow on us the Spirit of Truth to teach us; the Spirit of comfort to strengthen us; the Spirit of renewal that we may become as new creatures. O Spirit of God, sanctify us; Thou seest how full our hearts yet are of impurity, but Thou seest also our earnest desire to be made pure. We are heartily sorry that we have ever grieved Thee, and slighted Thy gentle admonitions; and we yield ourselves now to Thy holy guidance. Be Thou the energy of our lives, the consolation of our affections, the light of our understandings, the rest and strength of our wills, the beginning and end of our spiritual life. O make us holy through and through that we may be preserved without offence unto the day of Jesus Christ. Make our hearts a temple wherein Thou abidest; transform our members into the instruments of Thy righteousness. Lead us in a plain path unto heaven; assure us by Thy mighty witness that neither life nor death shall separate us from the love of God; abide continually within us, and witness with our spirits that we are His children. Sustain us in the hour of death, when all human help is of no avail, with the prospect of that glory which our Saviour hath gained for us. Amen.

Stark, 1740.

Tuesday Evening.

O MERCIFUL and gracious God and Father, we praise and thank Thee who hast divided the day from the night, the light from the darkness, and hast appointed the one for labour and the other for rest, that all Thy creatures may be refreshed therewith. We thank Thee for having permitted us to accomplish the past day under

Thy divine care and protection, and to surmount and cast behind us all the toil and troubles it has brought. Sufficient unto each day is its own burden. But Thou, O merciful Father, dost help us alway to bear each burden as it comes, till at last we shall reach Thy perfect rest and never-ending day, where troubles and weariness shall be no more. We thank Thee heartily for all the good things that we have received to-day from Thy hands; ah! Lord, we are not worthy of the mercies which Thou daily bestowest; and we thank Thee also for having averted the evil that might have befallen us, and kept us under the shadow of the Almighty from disaster and deadly sin. Heartily as Thy children we cry to Thee, forgive us all the sins we have committed this day in thought, deed, and word; for we have done much that is wrong, and neglected to do much that was right. Have mercy on us, O God, have mercy on us; let us die to sin and arise to become ever more God-fearing, more holy, just, and pious. Let our sleep be no sinful slumber, but may our thoughts and souls be still with Thee; may we speak unto Thee as we lie down and think of Thee as we awake, that sleeping or waking Thy Name be ever in our memories. Preserve us from all dangers and terrors of the night; from fearful dreams; from the attack of evil men; from perils of water and fire. Behold, He that keepeth Israel doth not slumber nor sleep; extend then Thy right hand over us, that in its shadow the sun may not smite us by day, neither the moon by night. Awaken us to-morrow in due time to serve Thee with all our powers, and promote Thy glory. But if in Thy inscrutable wisdom this night should prove to any one of us his last on earth, O grant him then to fall asleep in perfect rest in Jesus Christ our Lord. Amen.

J. Arndt, 1555–1621.

Wednesday Morning.

O LORD God, our Father, Lord of our Life! We thank Thee from the bottom of our hearts that Thou hast held the hand of Thy fatherly compassion over us during the past night, hast guarded us by Thy holy angels, and suffered us to arise again to Thy praise.

And we pray Thee, O most merciful Father, through Jesus Christ Thy Son, our Saviour, keep us this day in Thy grace, love, and care. Rule our thoughts and dispositions, our words and works by Thy Holy Spirit, that we may do nothing wrong nor offend against Thee. Lead us in the right way; suffer us more and more to enjoy the sense of Thy love, and make our hearts Thy dwelling-place and Thy temple. O Almighty God, Thou art our Father, we are Thy children; forsake us not, for on Thee have we depended from our earliest hour; our prosperity and adversity are in Thy hands alone. If it please Thee to-day to send us prosperity, give us also Thy aid to make good use of it; but if adversity should overtake us, enable us to bear it with patience. In Thy

Name we begin our daily occupations ; may we accomplish successfully whatsoever we have to do, through Thy strength, and fail not to render Thee hearty thanks for Thy help. Whatever benefits Thy goodness bestows on us may we receive with childlike contentment, and not crave for more or for forbidden things. Draw us away from the love of this world ; we will desire it not. And if trouble comes, be not Thou terrible unto us, O our God ; for if we have Thee, it is enough for earth or heaven ; though heart and flesh may fail, yet art Thou, O God, the Strength of our hearts and our Portion for ever. More precious art Thou than all the treasures of the earth ; let us never fall away from Thy blessed love. Abide with us to-day and for ever. To Thee we commend both our friends and foes ; bless the former, convert the latter. Have pity according to Thy great mercy on all the poor and destitute, all the sorrowful and comfortless. Be the eternal salvation of Thy Church ; and make us true and living members of the same, so that when we depart from this life we may be raised to Thee in Thy Heaven above. O Father, hear us, and grant our prayers in the Name of Thy Son Jesus Christ. Amen.

Lassenius, 1686.

Wednesday Evening.

O LORD God, our Father in Heaven, Lord of our life, Thy works are pure goodness and truth. Thou hast kept us in life this day, and hast shown us much loving-kindness, and preserved us from evil; therefore our mouth is full of Thy praise. But we are ashamed before Thee, O God, for we have once more sinned against Thee this day; we have not trod unswervingly in Thy path of duty. Ah, Lord, who can tell how oft he offendeth; forgive us even our secret faults. Help us to overcome them, O Thou Consolation of Israel, and dispel our misdeeds as a cloud, and our sins as the morning mist. Redeem us, and purify our consciences from dead works, through the cross of Thy Son Jesus Christ, and withdraw not Thy helping hand from us. Behold, O Blessed Father, the night is gathering fast, the darkness surrounds us; leave us not, O Thou who art our Light; go not down upon our hearts, O Thou our Sun! Watch over us and defend us, parents and children, our household and home, our health and wealth; and keep us from harm and danger. May we calmly rest on Thy unfathomable goodness, and may Thy Word be our lantern and our guiding star. Unto Thee we commend ourselves, for in Thee is our hope; continue to guard and succour our souls, and may we awake to-morrow, if it be Thy will, with joyful hearts ready to sing Thy praise. Hear us for Thy dear Son's sake. Amen.

Lassenius, 1686.

Thursday Morning.

WE bow our knees before the Father of our Lord Jesus Christ, who is the true Father of all who are called children in Heaven and earth; and we pray Him to give us power according to the riches of His glory, that we may be strengthened with might in the inner man; that Christ may dwell in our hearts by faith; and that we being rooted and grounded in love, may know with all saints the height and depth and breadth of Thy knowledge, which is better than all wisdom, and be filled from the fulness of God.

We acknowledge with thankful hearts this morning all Thy goodness, and will not hide Thy faithfulness, which Thou hast showed us from our cradle until this hour. Thou hast led us alway in the cords of love, and hast suffered us to sleep this night in safety and to rest in peace. And now shine Thou forth upon us like the glorious dawning from the East, descend upon us as the rain which watereth the earth. O God who causest the light to shine out of darkness, pour such clear light into our minds that we may behold Thee in the face of

Jesus Christ. Make us meet for the inheritance of the saints in light; help us to walk in Thy Name; be to-day our Salvation and the strength of our life, that we may fear no evil; for Thou art the Source of all life, and in Thy light shall we see light. Let us abide in the thought of Thy presence, that we may receive continual supplies of new strength, and mount up with wings as an eagle, and never faint nor grow weary in Thy service.

Give strength, O merciful Father, unto the sick; help the poor; comfort the afflicted; refresh the sorrowful; defend them that are ready to despair. Feed Thou the hungry; provide for the forsaken, and bless us also in our goings-out and comings-in. Lord Jesu Christ, help us through Thee to gain one victory after another over temptation, whether from the world, the evil one, or our own passions. O Holy Spirit, be our Light in darkness, our Teacher in ignorance, our Guide in all our ways, and renew our hearts according to Thy will. Make us Thy holy temple, O God, and let all we have and all whom we love, love Thee in sincerity and serve Thee with undivided hearts. Bless us in our daily work. Let our country, its government, and its people enjoy Thy protection in soul and body until we all reach Thy day of endless rest. And now unto Him who is able to do exceedingly abundantly for us beyond all we can ask or think of, be glory for ever and ever. Amen.

Lassenius, 1686.

Thursday Evening.

O BLESSED Lord, abide with us now, for the day is far spent, and the night is at hand. We cannot thank and magnify Thee enough, O God, for the love and faithfulness, the mercy and goodness which have followed us throughout this day; be Thou now through the night our ever-present Defender and Shield. We confess that we have given Thee cause to hide Thy face from us, for we have sinned much and often against Thee. Thou seest, O heavenly Father, that in us dwelleth no good thing; for even when to will is present with us, we often cannot do that which is right. But what we cannot do, our Redeemer hath done for us; where we have failed, He hath made amends. Accept Him, O God, as the Mediator between Thee and us, through whom we may be reconciled and at peace with Thee. And now, O Father, we would seek our rest; we entrust our souls and bodies to Thee, in sure confidence that they are safe in Thy keeping. When we sleep, do Thou watch over us; be our shield against the fiery darts of the wicked one, that no evil thoughts arise in our hearts. Let Thy fatherly arms be around us, that no harm may come nigh our dwelling. May we rest beneath the shadow of Thy wings, and say with David, 'We can lay us down and sleep in peace, for Thou, Lord, makest us to dwell in safety.' Amen.

Quirsfeldt, 1642–1686.

Friday Morning.

O LORD God, Heavenly Father, in this morning hour we commend ourselves in soul and body unto Thy gracious rule, Thy mighty protection, Thy fatherly providence and care. Let no evil befall us to-day, and no plague come nigh our dwelling. May Thy good Spirit so rule and dispose our hearts unto childlike obedience, that we may not swerve from the paths of true godliness and uprightness. Bless our household in its temporal wants; and in all our lawful business and undertakings, may Thy heavenly wisdom illuminate us, Thy energy strengthen us, Thy love constrain us, Thy fear be present with us, that we may walk in righteousness, remembering our covenant of baptism. May we treat all around us with gentleness, sincerity, humility, and active kindness, ever bearing in mind Thy command to do unto others as we would that they should do unto us. Preserve us in health of body and mind so long as we remain here. Grant that whatever time be now left us to live, we may employ it well, and as becometh Christians, to the glory of Thy Name, to the service of our fellow-creatures, and to our own improvement. O give us grace to remember that we are mortal, and raise our thoughts above things temporal unto that which is heavenly and eternal. Preserve us from all impatience and irritability, and when we have finished the course that Thou in mercy hast appointed us, give us grace to be ready and willing to resign all that is of this earth, and glad to depart to be with Jesus. Then fulfil unto us that precious promise, that unto the sheep who hear Thy voice and follow Thee Thou wilt give eternal life; that not one of them shall perish, and none shall pluck them out of Thy hand. So grant that neither angels nor principalities, princes nor powers, things present nor things to come, nor height nor depth, nor any other creature, may separate us from Thy love. Amen, O Lord Jesu Christ. Amen.

Scriver, 1629–1693.

Friday Evening.

O HOLY Father, who dwellest in the light eternal, and hast need of no man, for Thou alone canst be sufficient unto Thyself, Thou yet hast desired that we should know Thy blessedness, and serve and honour Thee. O Lord, Thy hands have formed us, and Thou hast sent us into this world, that we may walk in the way that leads to Heaven and Thyself, and may find a lasting rest in Thee who art the Source and Centre of our souls. Look in pity on us poor pilgrims in the narrow way; let us not go astray, but reach at last our true Home where our Father dwells. Thou hast called us with a holy calling to depart from the evil of the world. Therefore, O God of Israel, who didst guide Thy people of old through the deserts to Canaan, and didst give them food and strength by the way, even so guide and govern us from day to day, and bestow on us food and strength for body and soul, that we may journey on in peace.

O Thou who art Eternal Life, who camest to earth to lead us wanderers back to our true Fatherland and Thy glorious kingdom; what a weary way was Thine here in Thy poverty and humiliation, and yet now Thou sittest at the right hand of Thy heavenly Father! Thy word cannot deceive, and Thou hast said, where I am, there shall they be also whom Thou hast given me. Draw us then ever more powerfully away from sin, from the world, from all the weaknesses which hinder us from treading steadily and faithfully in Thy footsteps, along the way wherein Thou hast gone before us, until with Thee we reach the end and aim of our faith. Forgive us for having hitherto so often wavered or looked back, and let us henceforward march straight on in the way of Thy laws, cleaving to Thee alone, freed from dependence on that which is seen and temporal, and receiving from Thy fulness grace for grace. Help us to conquer all temptations, preserve us from stumbling and false steps. Let us use all diligence to make our election sure by walking worthily as in Thy sight, and may our last step be a safe and peaceful passage to the arms of Thy love, and the blessed fellowship of the saints in light. Hear us, O Lord Christ, and glorify Thy name in us that we may glorify Thee for ever and ever. Amen.

Tersteegen, 1731.

Saturday Morning.

THOU wilt pour forth water on the thirsting, O our God, and streams upon the dry places; Thou wilt pour down Thy Spirit upon all flesh. Suffer us then to be partakers of this most excellent Gift, and bestow it on us in abundant measure. Enlighten us unto eternal life, that we may know Jesus Christ aright; hallow our wills that we may wish and crave nothing but what pleases Thee; give us power and boldness to walk in Thy ways, to overcome the world, to resist sin, and to live as Thy true children. Make us fruitful in all good works, refresh us in the heat of temptation, and give us Thy inward witness that Thy grace is with us. Rest upon us, O Spirit of Wisdom, that we may be guided into eternal truth; preserve our hearts from error, and dispel in them the darkness of ignorance and self-love. Rest upon us, O Spirit of holy Fear, and confirm our minds so that we fall not into wilful sin. Rest upon us, O Spirit of Love, and chase all anger, envy, and bitter grudges from our souls. Be our Comforter in trial, when the billows go over our heads; be our Strength in the hour of weakness, and help us to control the desires of the flesh. Let us grow in faith and love, in hope, patience, and humility. See by how many temptations we are surrounded, and preserve us from giving way to them; show us the path wherein we should tread, for if we trust to our own impulses we shall go astray; but if Thou lead us we shall run in the way of Thy commandments. Our hearts lie open before Thee; enter now with Thy rich gifts, strengthen, stablish, settle them. Dwell in them and make them Thy temple, so shall we have the pledge of our sonship, and of our salvation. Depart not from us in the last hour, but give us then, O Lord, a glimpse of yonder glory, a foretaste of yonder happiness, which shall be ours when after conflict comes the crown, after sorrow fulness of joy. Amen.

Stark, 1740.

Saturday Evening.

PRAYER.

WE thank Thee, O heavenly Father, for Thy great goodness in allowing Thy holy Word to be so often and richly proclaimed for the encouragement of us poor sinners. Imprint and seal it, O God, in our hearts, that we may act by it, and live and die by it. Grant us to grow and increase day by day in the knowledge of Thee; and let this knowledge not be ours alone, but let it be spread abroad among other nations, that it may touch and water our hearts and those of all our fellow-men, even as the rain and the snow water and fertilise the earth. So may we learn to know Thee, the eternal God, aright, to call on Thee and to praise Thee; and grant us in whatever we do or leave undone to make Thy holy commandments our guiding rule; that being found as obedient children, we may become partakers at last of the eternal life and inheritance above, which hath been won for us by Jesus Christ.

O Thou all-sufficient God, Thou Highest and Only Good of all who trust in Thee; in Thee alone can our hearts find rest, and in Thy favour is our highest joy. Lord, if we have Thee we have enough. Thy favour is life. O how well is it with us, when Thou art gracious unto us, and speakest peace to our consciences. Keep us in this peace which passeth all understanding, and do good unto our souls. Strengthen us in all trials by the inner comfort of Thy Holy Spirit, for our light affliction which is but for a moment worketh for us an exceeding glory. There will come a time when Thou wilt call us to the place of perfect rest. O grant us there to behold Thy face in righteousness, and to be satisfied from Thy eternal fulness. Amen.

Deucer and Ritter, 1689.

PRAYERS FOR SPECIAL OCCASIONS.

Prayer for Advent Sunday.

O LORD God, heavenly Father, we thank Thee for Thy grace that Thou hast sent us Thy Son, and hast appointed Him to be the King of Righteousness, and our Saviour and Redeemer, who should rescue us from the dominion of darkness, and bestow on us righteousness, salvation, and blessedness. We pray Thee now to enlighten us with the knowledge of Him, and strengthen us in the true Christian faith, that we may accept and praise Him as our King and Saviour, and with all our talents and energies, all the health and wealth Thou hast given us, may serve and obey Him. May He take up His abode among us and within us, and may we ever continue in His kingdom and allegiance. Incline the hearts and wills of all princes and governors to open their gates unto the King of kings and Lord of Glory; may He enter into their lands, cities, and churches, to dwell there, and to rule and govern all things by His Word and Spirit. Restrain and check all influences that would close the door against Him and forbid Him to come in, while giving free entrance to antichrist, to false teachers, and dreamers. Bring their evil enterprises to nought. But show forth Thy power and mercy on all the poor sons of men who are bound in the fetters of superstition or the dreariness of unbelief, in idolatry, false doctrine, or utter careless ungodliness; may Christ now come also unto them, and set up among them His kingdom of light, truth, and righteousness. So shalt Thou, O Eternal Father, with Thy eternal Son and Thy Holy Spirit be praised and worshipped at all times and in all places evermore. Amen.

Riga Prayer Book, 1707.

Prayer for Christmas Day.

O ETERNAL Father of our Lord Jesus Christ, who hast so wondrously manifested to us in Him Thy tenderness and loving-kindness; we pray Thee now bestow on us Thy dear Son, as the most precious Christmas gift; that Christ may be formed in our hearts, and Thou mayest have pleasure in Thy children. Open Thy fatherly heart, and bestow on us this treasure spiritually, as Thou once gavest Him in bodily form to the whole world. May we partake truly of the benefits of His holy incarnation, by laying hold each and all of us on the blessedness and salvation He hath prepared and brought to us. O Blessed Jesus, stretch forth Thy holy hand to us from that cradle of old, and call us to Thee, for Thou camest to bring us to Thyself from a world of sadness and sin. Thou art our Hope and our Salvation; O kindle our hearts with the flame of that love which made Thee leave Thy glory for our poverty; let it make us hunger and thirst to receive Thee in spirit, so that nought may ever part us from Thee. Let Thine image be formed in us, in gentleness and humility, in patience, self-denial, and poverty of spirit, in obedience and faithfulness to the truth, in child-like purity of heart. Grace and truth came by Thee, O let them come unto us. Peace hast Thou brought, O bestow it upon us sinners. Thou wouldst save from sin, then save us. And since Thou beholdest the poorest and lowest, make us willing to follow Thee through poverty or scorn unto the Cross; content in sorrow or persecution to know the fellowship of Thy sufferings which began for Thee from Thy birth; so that at last we may also reign with Thee in Thy joy for evermore. We praise Thee, O Saviour. Amen.

G. Arnold, 1697.

Prayer for the last Day of the Year.

WE thank Thee, O Lord of Hosts, we thank Thee for all the goodness and the wondrous things Thou hast done unto us both in this past year and during the whole previous period of our lives. For although we must confess that we have all sinned in many and various ways, and have been disobedient to Thy laws, so that Thou mightest justly have dealt with us as we have dealt toward Thee, and judged us as we have deserved; yet is Thy mercy so great that Thou hast spared us, and turned away Thine anger from us; for Thou art not as man, Thou art God, the Holy One among us. It is of Thy mercy that we are not consumed, and Thy compassions have no end. Thou hast cast our sins behind Thee, and pardoned us freely; Thou hast healed all our infirmities, and preserved our life from destruction; Thou hast crowned us with goodness and mercy. Thou hast blessed us in the Church, the school, and the family, and guarded us from misfortune. Thou hast given us teachers of righteousness who have warned us to turn from all evil ways and amend our lives. Thou hast given grace and wisdom to our rulers, so that we have been able to lead our lives in peace and tranquillity, as becometh Christians. We cannot recount all the good that Thou hast done for us in body and soul, in house and home, in work and wealth, in the city and the field. Praised be God, the Father of our Lord Jesus Christ, Who hath blessed us with all spiritual blessings in heavenly places in Christ; Who hath given us rain from heaven and fruitful seasons, and hath filled our hearts with food and gladness. Bless the Lord, for He is kind, and His mercy endureth for ever. Let all whom the Lord hath redeemed, whom He hath delivered from trouble, and rescued out of their anxieties, say, Blessed be the Lord God for ever and ever, and let all people say Amen and Amen.

B. Albrecht, 1569–1636.

Prayer for New Year's Day.

O LORD Almighty God, day and night are Thine. Thou appointest unto the stars their courses, and makest winter and summer; in Thee we live and move, and have our being. To-day we are entering by Thy providence upon a new year; therefore we come anew before Thy face, and cry unto Thee, O God, that Thou wouldst incline Thine ear unto us and hear us. Enlighten us and give us new hearts that we may put off the old man with his lusts and errors, and put on the new man, which is according to Thy will in righteousness and true holiness. Give us grace to cast off all ungodliness, and put on the armour of light, and walk honestly as in the day; may we present our bodies and souls a living sacrifice unto Thee, which is our reasonable service. God be gracious to us; and bless us in the Church! Put Thy word into the mouths of our preachers, that they may joyfully proclaim Thy Gospel, and teach, comfort, warn, and reprove us with holy earnestness. Bless our rulers, and give them the fear of God and a good understanding, that they may govern well and wisely, and maintain peace and unity. Bless our homes; may husbands and wives be glad in each other; may parents have joy in their children, and children honour their parents; may brethren dwell in unity, and neighbours be kind one to another. Prosper us all with Thy blessing in our various callings and spheres, that we may be able to provide things honestly in the sight of all men, and may accomplish some useful work. Look on the tears of the widow and the orphan, listen to their cry, and despise not their complaint. Have mercy on all who are in any trouble or affliction, in pain or sickness, in trial and temptation. Help the poor, give them content, and make them rich in Thee. Guard the rich from pride and trusting in uncertain wealth, and teach them to look to Thee, the living God, Who canst alone continue them in the possession of what they enjoy. Heavenly Father, Thou knowest what we need for the true welfare of our children and ourselves; bestow on us then what we really want, and what will be good for us in time and eternity. Teach us to do what pleases Thee; let Thy good Spirit lead us in a plain path; may we hear Thy inner voice in our consciences and turn not aside from its commands to the right hand or the left. Convert those who are enemies unto Thee; bless all pious hearts who love Thee; and if, in the course of this year, Thou call any of us hence—for we know not what a day may bring forth—then, O Lord, show us Thy mercy, take us hence in peace, and let us calmly fall asleep in Thy dear Son our Saviour, Jesus Christ. Amen.

B. Albrecht, 1560–1636.

Another Prayer for New Year's Day.

(THE FEAST OF THE CIRCUMCISION.)

ALL praise to Thee, O dearest Saviour, for Thy wondrous redemption, which Thou didst begin as on this day, when Thou wast made subject to the law, and wast for the first time its victim. Thou didst then take the name of Jesus, wherein Thou didst promise to save Thy people from their sins. We thank Thee, O Lord, that Thou hast shown us afresh during the past year how well this name becomes Thee, for Thou hast saved us in the time of need, and hast rescued us from many a peril and temptation. Continue to be to us our living Jesus, our Saviour in word and deed. Deliver us above all from our spiritual enemies, from that Sin which is the bitterest and most deadly hurt. Wash away the unrighteousness of the old man, and renew us in the spirit of our hearts, that we may put on Thee, Lord Jesus, with all Thy grace and power, and with the new season may be made a new creature in Thee. Behold our heart longeth for Thy new creation wherein Thou wilt make all things new. So create a new spirit in us, that with the old one all things may pass away that have hitherto vexed and disturbed us, and hindered Thee from blessing us fully. O Jesus, revive with the changing year Thy memory in our hearts, that we may anew behold Thee by that faith which God himself implants. Be to us what Thy name imports—pure blessing and salvation. Give us with the new year new righteousness and sanctification, new wisdom and redemption. Let us begin this year with fresh resolve and earnestness, not in the old leaven of hypocrisy and wickedness, not in our old sins and habits. Oh that we may all now entreat of Thee a heart to fear Thee as children, to love Thee ardently, to cry to Thee fervently, to fight for Thee loyally! Let us cleave to Thy love, and seek Thy knowledge, and taste Thy sweetness in our hearts, that we may thirst every day and hour for Thee. Oh be Thou our all in all, for

in Thee lies all that we can need! Be to our rulers the true Law-book, through Thy holy Name, which is the Word of God; be their righteous sceptre, that Thy will alone may come to pass through them; be their defence and their shield, their reward and their crown. Be unto all teachers the Light which lighteneth every man, that will lead the wandering aright, instruct the ignorant, strengthen the weak, comfort the sad. Be to all congregations a holy temple, wherein they may assemble in the unity of the Spirit for mutual help and edification. Let Thy Name be as it hath ever been, the treasure of the poor, the healing of the sick, the refuge of the wretched, the counsel and hope of the forsaken, the provider of the widow, the father of the orphan, yea all things they need to all men. Thou heavenly Manna, give Thyself to each soul this year to enjoy, as it shall need and desire Thee, for Thou dost willingly bestow Thyself on all who seek and cry to Thee. Grant us the precious pearl of Thy kingdom, then have we enough for ever. Satisfy the hunger of our souls for Thee, and complete the work of redemption which Thou hast begun in us, then shall we crave nought else. For Thou canst awaken us from death, and give us new strength in our weakness, and change our anger into love, our curse into a blessing. Yea, teach us Thyself how to please Thee, and without Thee let us neither think, nor speak, nor do anything. We commend ourselves unto Thee wholly, with all we are and have, for ever and ever. Amen.

G. Arnold, 1697.

Prayers which may be used at any Time in Lent.

COLLECT.

BLESSED Lord, grant unto us Thy Holy Spirit to work in us daily a true and lasting repentance, and keep us ever as contrite Christian people, willing to acknowledge, bewail, and lament our sins; yet also, keep us ever, O Lord, steadfast and strong in our faith in the forgiveness of sins, and in our purpose to amend our lives, through Jesus Christ our Lord. Amen.

Eichhorn, 1546.

PRAYER I.

O LORD our God, in Whom is the fulness of all true good, what are we that we should presume to speak to Thee? We are the least of Thy servants, far poorer and more unprofitable than we ourselves are aware or dare to acknowledge. Yet, O Lord, remember that in ourselves we are, have, and can do nothing, and Thou alone art good, just, and holy, almighty and fulfillest all things. Only the wilful sinner wilt Thou leave empty, only into his heart canst Thou not enter. Then think upon Thy mercy, and fill our hearts with Thy presence; for how shall we endure in this evil world unless Thy grace and mercy give us strength? Hide not Thy face from us; tarry not to visit Thy creatures; take not Thy comfort from us, that our souls be not as the parched unfruitful land. Lord, teach us to do Thy will; to walk humbly and justly before Thee; for Thou art our wisdom, Thou knowest us in very truth, ere ever we beheld the light; Thou knowest and canst heal all our infirmities. Amen.

Riga Prayer Book, 1701.

PRAYER II.

O GREAT and infinite God, we come before Thy face, though we are unworthy to do so, and pray that Thou wouldst Thyself show us how faithless we have been to Thy grace. We are the Prodigal Son who hath wasted his portion of his Father's goods; and now in our distress we have no refuge but to fly to Thee, and own that we have sinned against Thee, and have been deaf and blind to Thy kingdom. What then shall we say unto Thee, O Thou Judge of all flesh? We are poor and destitute, we can but plead the infinite compassion which Thou hast revealed in the death of Thy Son. For the sake of His sufferings and death have mercy upon us, and set our souls free from the heavy fetters of sin wherein we are bound. Accept us in the inexhaustible loving-kindness which Thou openest to all repentant sinners, redeem us from sin, save us from death, and above all from our own wills which have separated us from Thee. We cannot in our own strength change ourselves and make ourselves good, help us therefore to overcome our sins by Thy strength; draw us to Thy Son, who has given Himself for us, that we may be delivered from the snares of our enemy Sin, and experience Thy salvation in Christ. Oh awaken us from the death of carelessness unto a new and vivid life; turn our hearts, minds, and inclinations entirely to Thyself, that from this moment onwards we may forsake the vain things of Time, and be transformed, and live in very deed. Bestow on our poor thirsting souls Thy hidden energy, which can constrain all men with its healing grace, so shall we be purified, comforted, and satisfied with blessing. Help us, by Thy Cross and death. O Lord our God we cast ourselves wholly on Thee for our redemption; yea, we will not let Thee go until Thou bless us. Amen.

G. Arnold, 1697.

PRAYER III.

RIGHTEOUS art Thou, O Lord, and upright is Thy judgment; yea, all Thy judgments are righteous and true. Therefore we humbly cry to Thee, that Thou shouldst not deal with us according to our sins which deserve Thy punishment, but according to Thy great mercy which pardons all them that repent. Have mercy upon us, and help us according to the love wherewith Thou hast loved us in Christ Thy Son, and admit us to Thy grace, through the merits of our Saviour.

We acknowledge our wickedness unto Thee; we will not hide how heavily we are burdened with sin. Our errors are more than we can count, and our transgressions are many. Whither shall we go, O God, if Thou wilt not turn to us? Where shall we hide ourselves if Thou art not gracious to us, and wilt not have pity on us? Chastise us, but forgive us; punish us, but let us not perish. Though a mother may forget her child, yet wilt Thou not forget us, O Father. Therefore we cry to Thee and come before Thy face, and our complaint hopeth for a merciful answer.

We have sinned, our consciences condemn us, and our repentance cannot make amends to Thy justice. We cannot stand on that day when Thou wilt bring the works of all men into judgment, and wilt reward every man according to what he hath done. Then must we be dumb, while our sin bears witness and our iniquity rises up against us. Then will all our boasting be vain, and if we would justify ourselves, the testimony of Thine Omniscience would condemn us.

But Thou, O Lord, willest not the death of a sinner, but rather that he should be converted and live. Thou didst send Jesus Christ that all who believe in Him should not perish, but have everlasting life. In His death shall they live again, and receive reconciliation, and be assured of forgiveness. Therefore we come to Thee, and place our trust in Thee, and hope for Thy helping grace.

We are bidden to seek Thee, O Lord, and Thou wilt suffer us to find Thee. When we call upon Thee, Thou hast promised to hear us. See, we knock, that Thou shouldst open to us, and let Thy countenance shine upon us. Be gracious unto us when we give ourselves up into Thy hand. When we approach Thee with all our sins, reject us not. Accept us and draw us to Thee, that we may be Thine now and for ever, who livest and reignest evermore.

We commend ourselves to Thee, O Father, and to the gracious influence of Thy Holy Spirit. Watch over our senses and our thoughts, root out all pride in us, and give us humility and contrition of heart. Teach us to do according to Thy will, and let us know the depth of Thy mercy. If Thy strength uphold us, we shall live, but without Thee we can do nothing. If Thou healest us our souls are made whole; if Thou sendest us Thy light, darkness shall not have dominion over us.

Look down upon us, O Lord, from the abode

of Thy glory, and let all the darkness of our souls vanish before the beams of Thy brightness. Fill us with holy love, and open to us the treasures of Thy wisdom. All our desire is known unto Thee, therefore perfect what Thou hast begun, and what Thy Spirit has awakened us to ask in prayer. We seek Thy face, turn Thy face unto us and show us Thy glory. Then shall our longing be satisfied, and our peace shall be perfect. Amen.

St. Augustine.

A Collect to be used before any of the former Prayers during Passion Week.

WE thank Thee with our whole heart, O beloved Father, for the precious blood of Thy dear Son, which He hath shed for our sakes; wherewith Thou yet daily cleansest, quickenest, and sanctifiest us in Thy holy Church, and makest us partakers of Thy divine nature. We thank Thee for the great and unspeakable love wherewith Thou hast loved us, though we were not worthy of it; in that Thou hast redeemed us by Thine own Son, who is our High-priest and Mediator, the true Shepherd Who yielded up His life for the sheep of His flock, Who now sits on Thy right hand and intercedes for us. And we implore and entreat Thee, O good and faithful God, Thou Friend of all mankind, give us Thy grace, that for all this Thy great compassion, we may praise Thee with Thy Son and the Holy Spirit, in every act of our lives, evermore. Amen.

St. Augustine.

On the Institution of the Lord's Supper.

O DEAREST Lord Jesus, how shall we sufficiently praise and thank Thee for the unspeakable love and kindness which Thou hast shown us on this day. To-day Thou beginnest that weary way, whereon Thou wilt patiently make atonement by Thy own bitter sorrows for the sins of the whole world. Yet before Thou enterest upon it, Thou dost make a covenant with us in Thy blood that is shed for those sins. O sacred Covenant! O holy Testament! wherein Thou dost so give Thy sacred Body and Thy precious Blood as pledges of Thy love, that whosoever eateth Thy Flesh and drinketh Thy Blood shall dwell in Thee and Thou in him. Yea, Thou dost promise him eternal life, and Thou wilt raise him up at the last day to life everlasting. O grant, Blessed Jesus, that we may never slight the precious Feast of love, of which Thy disciples partook for the first time this day, but may lay it to heart with true reverence. May we always partake of it with deep-felt devotion and sincere faith; and grant that it may ever be duly administered among us according to Thy Word and primitive ordination; so that we, as Thy Apostle teaches us, when we eat of this bread and drink of this cup, may show forth Thy death till Thou comest to raise us from this sorrowful world to Thy glory, where we shall sit at Thy table, and be filled with the abundance of Thy house. Amen.

Quirsfeld, 1642-1686.

Prayer for Good Friday.

O THOU spotless Lamb of God, Who hast borne all our sins upon the Cross, have mercy upon us now and evermore. We sinners bow in deep humility before Thy holy Face, as Thou hangest on the Cross for our sakes, and lay our confession at Thy feet.

For, O Thou Holy One, Thou sufferest not

for Thy own misdoings; we, we are the cause of Thy sorrow and pains. We have done amiss; we have sinned, O Lord, and deserved God's judgments. We have sinned through forgetfulness of Thy just and holy ways. We have sinned through false love of the world and a sinful love of self, for we have prized not Thee but the good things Thou hast given us. We have sinned in our wills, when they have set themselves against Thee, and we have acted according to our own conceits and not hearkening to Thy inner voice. We have sinned in resisting Thy Holy Spirit by our neglect of so many precious means of grace, and have not brought forth the fruits for the sake of which Thou didst bestow them. We have sinned in careless and ungodly acts, in unnecessary and sinful words, in vain longings which have led us away from Thee. All these and countless other conscious and unconscious sins of ours hast Thou borne, O Lamb of God; yea, our sins and the sins of the whole world; therefore sorrow pressed so hard upon Thee, that in the deep anguish of Thy heart, Thou wast forced to cry, O God, my God, why hast Thou forsaken me! So didst Thou suffer that we might not be forsaken for ever by the joy-inspiring countenance of our God. O Jesu, Thou Son of

The Most High God, Thyself God from evermore! who can fathom the wondrous mysteries of Thy sufferings, that Thou, the Eternal Son, Thou shouldst for our sakes take such deep and awful suffering on Thyself, to gain for us a full and perfect redemption? May those woes of Thine be afresh imprinted on our hearts, that we may glorify Thy love not only with our lips, but in spirit and in truth, by surrendering ourselves and all that we have to Thy service.

And let Thy sorrows soften our hearts anew to contrition and repentance; let the sight of them inspire us with a deep aversion to all sin, even the most trifling. O that at least from henceforward we may lay no further burden upon Thee, nor crucify Thee afresh! Fill us with an abiding sense of the evil of sin and the holiness of God which are manifested in Thy Cross, with a holy fear of the Divine majesty now, so that hereafter we may appear without fear before God, as our God. Bring us into the true fellowship of Thy Passion, Cross, and Death, that we may die with Thee to the world and its lusts, sin and her vanities, and may show our poor gratitude by willingly offering the best and dearest that we have, at Thy feet Who hast given us so infinitely much. Lord, let Thy steadfastness on the Cross make us steadfast in all inward and outward trial, that having followed Thee faithfully in the way of the cross here, we may at last be made conquerors with Thee and heirs of Thy heavenly kingdom. Yea, Lord Jesu, let us follow Thee whithersoever Thou goest. Thou as our Mediator wilt guide us back to God. Lead us by the hand through the darkness of this evil world, that we may choose and keep to the right path, the path of deadness to self and sin, and true hearty prayer, so that by Thee, our only Leader and Way, we may be brought in living faith to God, even our God and Father, and may penetrate into the sanctuary of His innermost and eternal communion.

Bless all who are Thine; suffer none to be lost; keep all those whom Thou hast purchased with Thy blood, and let our souls be precious in Thy sight. Sustain all lonely and heavy-laden hearts. Bless Thy whole Zion, the flock of Thy pasture. Be Thy love ever near us, so that at last we may attain eternal joy. Hear us, O Lord! hear our prayers; not for our worthiness, but for Thy free mercy and the glory of Thy great Name. Amen.

Tersteegen, 1731.

Collect for Easter Sunday.

THOU merciful and loving and faithful Lord Jesus Christ, Who hast died for our sins and art risen again for our justification, we pray Thee, by Thy holy resurrection, that Thou wilt awaken us also from the grave of sin and wickedness, and give us Thy grace, that at the resurrection of the dead we may be partakers of Thy resurrection. Amen.

Or this.

THOU Son of the Living God, Who, as the true Bread of Life, dost feed and satisfy with Thy body and blood all sorrowful souls, and aching consciences, and hungering and thirsting hearts, Who dost moreover invite and bid every man to this heavenly feast, accept us also in Thy grace, feed and quicken our poor souls with Thy body and blood unto eternal life. Amen.

St. Augustine.

Prayer for Easter Sunday.

O PRINCE of Life, Lord Jesu Christ, we worship Thee in Thy power and glory, wherein Thou hast triumphed over Death and Hell, over Thy enemies and ours. To Thee, O mighty Prince of Peace and Life, will we give honour; to Thee will we pay homage as our Lord and King; to Thee will we yield ourselves with all we are and have. Heaven and earth must worship Thee, and all things bring Thee praise. Have mercy, O Lord, upon us, and help us in the day of resurrection; let not Thy conflict and Thy victory be in vain for us. Let us know, by our own experience, that Thou livest and reignest, and art present to help us. Oh, we lead our life too much in our own strength, trusting to our own poor weak efforts, because we give not space for Thee to work and speak within us! Imprint it deeply on our hearts that we must not be negligent in prayer, but must continually cleave to Thee and wait upon Thee, and look for the quickening influence of Thy Spirit. Draw us from the grave up to Thy own life. Let what is seen and temporal become ever of less account in our eyes; while Thy Divine Life becomes ever more truly felt in our hearts, ever dearer and mightier, until we learn to live as pilgrims and strangers in this world. Turn away our thoughts from whatsoever doth not belong to Thy kingdom; let our whole conduct show that we are Thine own, and have Thee for our Lord.

O Lord, we acknowledge Thy dominion over us; our life, our death, our soul and body, all belong to Thee. O grant that we may willingly consecrate them all to Thee, and use them in Thy service.

Let us walk before Thee in childlike simplicity, steadfast in prayer; looking ever unto Thee, that whatsoever we do or abstain from we may in all things follow the least indications of Thy will. Become Lord of our hearts and spirits; that the whole inner man may be brought under Thy rule, and that Thy life of love and righteousness may pervade all our thoughts and energies and the very ground of our souls; that we may be wholly filled with it. Come, O Lord and King, enter into our hearts, and live and reign there for ever and ever.

O faithful Lord, teach us to trust Thee for life and death; to take Thee for our All in All; and may we enter with Thee into Thy everlasting kingdom. Hear us, O Lord Christ, according to the riches of Thy grace, and for the glory of Thy great Name. Amen.

Tersteegen, 1731.

Prayer for Easter Sunday.

(EVENING.)

O THOU kind and gracious Easter King who didst as to-day comfort and guide into the right way Thy two sorrowing and erring disciples; we confess and acknowledge that our understanding in what the prophets have taught is by nature dark even as theirs, and that in spiritual things we can accomplish nothing good of ourselves. We, therefore pray Thee to come to the aid of our weakness and blindness, to make us fervent in faith and ardent in love, that the light of Thy knowledge may spring up in our hearts. And since the last hour draweth on, and the evening is at hand, and the day is far spent on this earth, and Thy dear Christian Church is sorely beset on all sides by unbelievers and misbelievers, by false brethren, by the world and her mighty ones; oh, therefore, abide with us, O Lord! hasten to our aid, O Lord our Help! And when the evening of our life is at hand, then abide with us and in us, that so we may pass hence with joy to that place where we shall abide with Thee for ever. Amen.

St. Augustine.

Prayer for Ascension Day.

O SAVIOUR, Who in love to us didst empty Thyself of Thy glory and take upon Thee the form of a servant, and becamest obedient unto the death upon the Cross; behold, God hath given Thee a Name which is above every name. Let the power of Thy glory be made known to our hearts, that we also may bow to Thy Name, and be true and loyal to Thee our King.

We thank Thee, O Lord, that by Thy ascension Thou hast paved the way to Heaven for us, and opened to us Thy Father's heart. Thou sittest at the right hand of the Majesty of God, that all hearts may be subject to Thee as their rightful King. Behold! here are hearts over which Thou shouldst reign as sovereign Lord; O send down a glance of loving-kindness upon us. Give us a heavenly mind. May we be kept by Thy grace from the vanities of earth; make us feel Thy presence, and grow still and calm beneath Thy gracious influence, and happy in the light of Thy countenance. Thou who hast the true key of knowledge, open our eyes to behold the greatness of Thy glory and the abundance of Thy love, that we may at once begin to turn our thoughts and hearts heavenwards, to live a holy life as in Thy sight, and to love Thee who hast so loved us, and art so infinitely worthy of our love. O Lord, forgive us, for Thy mercy's sake, for having so often heard of Thee and Thy ascension, and yet experienced so little of its power in our souls. Glorify Thyself now in us; teach us to know Thee in all Thy greatness, to love and honour Thee. Make our hearts Thy dwelling; work in them a faith and joyful courage which will enable us to follow Thee, Who hast gone before us, and hast attained the goal.

Hear our weak prayers, O great High-priest above; and gain us, by Thy merits, a mighty Yea and Amen. Amen.

Tersteegen, 1731.

Whit Sunday.

COLLECT.

O GOD the Holy Ghost, who being of one essence with the Father and the Son, dost ever proceed from them, and didst descend on the Lord Christ in the form of a Dove, and on His disciples in that of fiery tongues; we thank Thee, we praise Thee, and entreat that Thou wouldst chase from our souls all the darkness of evil, and kindle in them the light of Thy grace and the fire of Thy love, Who livest and reignest, true God, for ever and ever. Amen.

St. Augustine.

PRAYER.

O GOD, Who, on the holy day of Pentecost, didst so graciously and bounteously endue the hearts of Thy faithful servants with Thy Holy Spirit, O shed Thy Spirit like a tender rain on our dry and perishing hearts; quicken Thy heritage; refresh the sorrowful. Come, O Holy Spirit, and adorn us with Thy manifold gifts, that we also may truly acknowledge and praise the great deeds which God hath wrought in Jesus Christ, that with new tongues we may proclaim and glorify and spread abroad Thy Word. Kindle us with the flame of Thy sacred ardour; burn out of us all inward evil, all sinful desires and lusts of the flesh; show us the light of Thy Truth, that we may fervently serve our God with the right zeal and earnestness. O Thou God of Peace, unite our hearts by Thy bond of peace, that we may live with one another continually in gentleness and humility, in peace and unity. O Thou God of Patience, give us patience in the time of trial, and steadfastness to endure to the end. O Thou Spirit of prayer, awaken our hearts, that we may lift up holy hands to God, and cry unto Him in all our distresses; and since we know not what to ask for, nor how to ask aright, O plead for us as our faithful Intercessor with sighings that cannot be uttered. O Thou gentle Wind, cool and refresh our hearts in all heat and anguish. Be our Defence and Shade in the time of need, our Help in trial, our Consolation when all things are against us. Come, O Thou mighty God, strengthen the weak, teach the ignorant Thy way, raise up those that have fallen, bring back the erring, and confirm them by Thy right hand. Come, O Thou eternal Light, Salvation, and Comfort, be our Light in darkness, our Salvation in life, our Comfort in death; and lead us in the straight way to everlasting life, that we may praise Thee, with our heavenly Father and His beloved Son our only Saviour, in the true Pentecost of eternity, for ever and ever. Amen.

B. Albrecht, 1569–1636.

Prayer for Trinity Sunday.

O FATHER of lights, and Giver of all good and perfect gifts, we beseech Thee to give us all things that are good for us, even such things as we have not yet learnt to acknowledge and desire as good; but above all give us Thyself, Who art the eternal and highest Good of all Thy creatures. Produce in us true faith, together with a sincere repentance, a changed heart, and a life wholly renewed to Thee. Give us faith, O Father, to find in Thee an all-sufficient Protection, a tender Comforter, a compassionate Father, a Hope that cannot be shaken, an eternal Rock of salvation. Grant us so to taste the sweetness of Thy love to us, that we may love Thee in return, may obey Thee freely from affection not from constraint, and be rich in love like Thine to all our fellow-men. Govern our thoughts, hallow our wills, restrain our lips and our senses by Thy holy fear. Strengthen in us a vivid hope in the life that is to come; breathe into us an ardent devotion; and let us find access to Thee, and feel that in prayer we are drawing close to our Father's heart.

O Lord Jesu Christ, be Thou now and

evermore, by Thy deliverance from all sin, our mighty Helper; by Thy word of wisdom, our Master and Teacher; and by Thy spiritual advent, our ever-present Emmanuel and our living Saviour. Transform our hearts into Thine image of gentleness and humility; and let us ever bear Thee and Thy love to us in mind. Through Thy sorrows and Thy resurrection be Thou to us in very deed Light, Life, and Strength; our Refuge and Rest; our Mediator, and whatsoever else we may need. Come and reign in us as a King; instruct us as a Prophet; plead for us and within us as our High-priest; and so take full possession of us as the true Light of our souls.

O Holy Spirit, lighten our darkness, purify our impurity, strengthen our weakness, comfort us in sorrow, give us life in death. Make us fervent in spirit, joyful in hope, patient in affliction. Teach us to be persevering in prayer, gentle under provocation, humble alike in honour and contempt. Be our Interpreter in the study of Thy word, our Counsellor in doubt, our Leader in uncertainty, our Help at need, our Life in death, our Guide and unfailing Companion to our true Home with God in Heaven. Amen.

G. Arnold, 1697.

A Prayer that may be used in time of Bereavement, or other Trial.

O MOST faithful and compassionate Father, we confess our sins before Thee; we own that we have merited more sorrow than we have received; and we rebel not against Thy righteous Providence. Yet look on us in mercy, and to all sorrowing hearts in this world be Thou a very present Help and Refuge, through Thine almighty goodness, whereon we now cast ourselves in faith. Reveal to us Thy mighty Presence in all the circumstances of our lot, save us thus from sinking under its troubles, and lead us in the right way, that these sufferings may be wholesome unto our souls. Be Thou the comfort of our hearts, when they mourn and are dismayed; speak gently unto us when we are overwhelmed with sorrow, and fear presses hard upon us. Save us from the terrors of death by the risen life of Thy Son; and when this bitter hour is past, let us once more draw breath and life from Thy quickening Spirit. Suffer us not to gaze abroad in search of earthly and transient consolations, which may lead us to forget Thee, and will but make our sorrow deeper at the end; but let Thy

Holy Spirit impel us to faith and prayer, to patience and hope, that we may receive Thy chastisements as children, and become better and holier thereby. So shall we learn to set our affections on Thee and Thy Truth, and be willing to part with what is only temporal.

Bless to us all Thy providence; purify the temple of our hearts through the holy fire of Thy cross, and make us worthy to suffer somewhat for Thy sake. And the harder our trial, the nearer be Thou, O God, with Thy comfort and strength; let us continually feel and enjoy them in our inmost souls, until, like gold and silver tried by the fire, we are made meet to enter into Thy kingdom, through our great Forerunner and pitying High-Priest. Amen.

G. Arnold, 1697.

A Prayer in time of Anxiety or Danger.

O ALMIGHTY God and Father, Thou Who art rich in help, our only comfort and refuge, Thou knowest and seest that we are now in great trouble and danger, and know not where to find counsel, or help, or consolation. It stands not in our power to save ourselves in this emergency; we know not what is best to do, but our eyes are fixed on Thee, Whose name is the Lord of Hosts, rich in counsel and mighty in deed, Whose hand hath spread abroad the heavens and prepared the dry land.

O God, our God, the billows are high and very tempestuous, but Thou art higher and greater; Thou art our only confidence in the troubles that have come upon us. Hast Thou not said by the mouth of Thy servant David: 'Though the earth be removed, and the mountains be carried into the midst of the sea; though the waters thereof roar and be troubled, and the mountains shake with the swelling thereof, yet shall the city of God be glad with her streams, the holy place of the Most High; for God is in the midst of her, therefore shall she not be moved.' Ah Lord, we bring Thy promise before Thee; Thou hast said: 'Seek ye My face,' therefore we seek Thy face; hide it not from us, turn not away from Thy children in anger, for Thou art our help. Take not away Thy hand from us, O God of our salvation, for all other aid hath forsaken us; do Thou take us up. We will yet hope to behold the goodness of the Lord in the land of the living; let us then be of good courage and undismayed, and wait on the Lord. Thy mercies cannot be exhausted, Thy promise cannot have come to an end; Thou canst not have forgotten to be gracious or shut up Thy loving-kindness in displeasure; Thy arm is not shortened, but is mighty to save; Thou art the God who dost wondrous things and showest Thy power among the people. Comfort us, then, O God our Saviour, and be not angry with us for ever. Wilt Thou not once more quicken us, that Thy people may rejoice in Thee? Lord, turn unto us, and be gracious to Thy servants; fill us early with Thy grace; refresh us after the days wherein we have been vexed and suffered calamity; be merciful unto us, and prosper the work of our hands. O Lord our God, send us help in this time of our need, for vain is the help of man. Thou hast said: 'In trouble shall he call upon my name, and I will hear him; with long life will I satisfy him, and show him my salvation.' Ah Lord, our misdeeds have deserved Thy wrath, yet help us for Thy name's sake, O Thou the Comfort of Israel, and her Deliverer. Thou art yet in our midst, and we are called by Thy name; O forsake us not, so shall we bring unto Thee a sacrifice of joy, and praise Thy name because it is so comfortable. Amen.

G. Arnold, 1697.

A Thanksgiving for Deliverance, which may be used after any of the former Prayers.

WE thank Thee, O God, with our whole hearts, and bless Thy name for ever and ever; Thou hast done all things well. We were in sorrow, and saw no light; then Thou hast had pity on us that we perished not. We cried to Thee in our trouble, and Thou didst hear our voice; our cry entered into Thine ears, and Thou didst comfort us; Thou hast stood beside us in faithfulness, and as a Father hast Thou rescued us from the waves of our great affliction.

O Lord and God, how shall we thank Thee for all the benefits that Thou daily showerest upon us. We will take the cup of salvation, and call upon the name of the Lord. His praises shall always be on our lips. Help us, O faithful God, to keep this vow; govern, guide, and lead us, that we may daily grow in gratitude and love to Thee, through Thy dear Son, our Lord and Saviour Jesus Christ; Who with Thee and the Holy Spirit ever liveth and reigneth, one God, world without end. Amen.

B. Albrecht, 1569-1636.

Collects

THAT MAY BE USED WITH ANY OF THE FORMER PRAYERS.

I.

ALMIGHTY and Eternal God, Who hast implanted in all Thy creatures a longing to be redeemed in Thee from the service of vain and transient things, and a waiting expectation for the glorious manifestation of Thy children; we pray Thee, enkindle by Thy grace in us, to whom Thou hast given the first-fruits of the Spirit, ever more of such holy and ardent desire after perfect union with Thyself, and complete enjoyment of that glorious freedom to which thou hast called us; through Jesus Christ, Thy dear Son our Lord. Amen.

II.

ALMIGHTY and Eternal God, Who dost bid us walk as pilgrims and strangers in this passing world, seeking that abiding city which Thou hast prepared for us in heaven; we pray Thee so to govern our hearts by Thy Holy Spirit, that we, avoiding all fleshly lusts which war against the soul, and quietly obedient to the government which Thou hast set over us, may show forth Thy glory before the world by our good works; for Jesus Christ's sake, Thy Son our Lord. Amen.

III.

ALMIGHTY and Eternal God, Who hast graciously bestowed on us the clear light of Thy Word, whereby we, notwithstanding our sins, can attain through Christ a childlike trust in Thee; we humbly pray Thee give us Thy Holy Spirit, that we may trust Thy Word with our whole hearts, and relying wholly upon Thee, may deny the world and ourselves, and bear the Cross after Thy dear Son in steadfast patience, through the same Jesus Christ our Lord. Amen.

IV.

ALMIGHTY and Eternal God, Who hast revealed Thy nature in Christ Jesus Thy Son as Love: we humbly pray Thee give us Thy Holy Spirit, that He may glorify Thee also in our hearts as pure Love, and thus constrain us by His Divine power to love Thee again with our whole souls, and our brethren as ourselves; that so by Thy grace we may be fulfilled with love, and evermore abide in Thee and Thou in us, with all joyfulness, and free from fear or distrust, through Jesus Christ our Lord. Amen.

V.

ALMIGHTY and Eternal God, by Whose free grace we are what we are, and by Whose undeserved mercy in Christ Jesus we have whatsoever in us is pleasing in Thy sight; we pray Thee let Thy Holy Spirit imprint this truth so powerfully on our hearts, that we may never, through presumptuous arrogance and self-conceit, sit in unloving and scornful judgment on our neighbour, but ever show the like mercy unto him, in all love and gentleness: through Jesus Christ, Thy dear Son our Lord. Amen.

VI.

ALMIGHTY and Everlasting God, Thou Lover of peace and concord, Who hast called us in Christ to love and unity: we pray Thee so rule our hearts by Thy Holy Spirit, that we, being delivered by the true fear of God from all fear of man, may evermore serve thee in righteousness, mercy, humility, and gentleness towards each other, through Thy dear Son Jesus Christ our Lord. Amen.

VII.

ALMIGHTY, Eternal God, Who dost so heartily desire our salvation, and dost so faithfully warn us in manifold ways to think in earnest on the things that belong to our peace; we pray Thee humbly give us Thy good Spirit, that we may believe in this Thy great love and faithfulness with our whole hearts, and may not trifle away our time of grace, but follow Thy voice which bids us come to Thee, while it is yet to-day: for the sake of Thy dear Son Jesu Christ our Lord. Amen.

VIII.

ALMIGHTY and Everlasting God, Who hast placed us in this life full of trials and tears, in order that we through
...same may learn to give careful heed to Thy
..., and be made meet for Thy kingdom:
...y Thee let Thy good Spirit dispose our
...o seek in Thy dear Son our only con-
...nder all sorrows, and enable us to forget
... and pain in the enjoyment of His
...love, through the same Jesus Christ
...Amen.

IX.

ALMIGHTY, Eternal God, Who hast placed us in this life full of temptations and conflicts, and hast armed us against them with the sword of faith in Thy Son, so that we in the power of His strength may, like Him, overcome the world and its mighty ones; we pray Thee give us Thy good Spirit, that He may establish us firmly in such faith and grace, and that we may abide steadfast in the same unto our life's end: through Jesus Christ our Lord. Amen.

X.

ALMIGHTY, Eternal God, Who in Jesus Christ Thy Son wilt heal us from the sickness of sin and death, and restore to us our lost spiritual health; we pray Thee give us Thy Holy Spirit, that through Him we may know Thy Son with our hearts, and all the inexhaustible fulness of Divine energy which dwelleth in Him; that we may before all things willingly follow the voice of our Heavenly Physician, and bow in childlike obedience beneath the operation of His gracious hand; through the same Jesus Christ our Lord. Amen.

XI.

ALMIGHTY, Eternal God, Who hast by Thy dear Son destroyed the power of Death, and brought life and immortality to light; we entreat Thee humbly, deliver us by Thy grace from all fear of death, and awaken in us by Thy Spirit an inward desire to depart and be with Christ, that so we may evermore in true faith, righteous holiness, and joyful hope, look forward to the glorious appearing of Jesus Christ, through the same Thy dear Son, our Lord. Amen.

After the Holy Communion.

IN remembrance, O Holy Father, of Thy unspeakable love and Thy Divine commandment, we bring Thee thanks, not as we ought, but as we can, and present ourselves unto Thee as a living sacrifice, through Jesus Christ; this sinful body, that it may be consecrated by Thy power to be an instrument of righteousness, and a temple of the Holy Ghost; this soul and this spirit, that Thou Thyself with Thy Son mayst abide therein; this heart, that Thy peace may reign in it, and the fire of Thy Divine love may fill it, to the destruction and consuming of all self-will, all anger and hatred, and all ungodly passions in us; finally, this mortal life, with all the gifts and faculties that we have received from Thy fatherly goodness, that they being sanctified by Thy grace may serve alone Thy will and glory; that so we, by Thy Divine working within us, may be fashioned into the Body of Thy dear Son. For His sake, O Lord our Heavenly Father, we firmly trust that Thou wilt now look on us with grace, and accomplish by Thy Holy Spirit this offering of ourselves. Amen.

Richard Rothe, 1846.

PRAYERS.

PART II.

Prayers and Meditations for Private Use.

"*Enter into thy closet, and when thou hast shut thy door, pray unto thy Father which is in secret.*"

PRAYERS AND MEDITATIONS

FOR PRIVATE USE.

I.

For Devotion in Prayer.

OH Lord, Thou just and holy God, Thou hast no pleasure in them who pray without real devotion; yet must I confess that I ought to be reckoned among their number, since I too often repeat my prayers, while my thoughts are busy with alien and unprofitable things, and my coldness of feeling allows no true fervour to enter my heart. O forgive me this fault in Thy mercy, most merciful Father; and kindle my heart henceforth to glowing and ardent devotion, that I may come before Thy face with trembling awe, and yet at the same time lift up my prayer to Thee with joyfulness. Give me the Spirit of Prayer, who will not only teach me to pray aright, but will Himself pray and cry Abba Father within my soul. Let my prayer be no mere muttering of the lips, but a fervent adoring sigh, welling forth from the inmost depth of my heart, and mounting on the wings of faith straight to Thy fatherly heart ; so shall I also obtain that gracious answer which Thy dear Son hath promised to all who ask in His Name. Amen. Grant me this, O Lord Jesu. Amen.

Quirsfeld, 1642-1686.

II.

Against the Neglect of Private Prayer.

O LORD God, Heavenly Father, Thou hast commanded me to pray ; Thy dear Son hath taught me how to pray, and hath given me a sacred promise that I shall be heard ; Thy Holy Spirit within me often puts me in mind of prayer. I know, moreover, that every good and perfect gift must come down from Thee, O Father of lights ; I know that no true, lasting, and profitable good, whether it be earthly or heavenly, temporal or eternal, can be attained without prayer. I know, too, that prayer concerns Thy glory, and is demanded by my great need ; I know what an intimate communion prayer is with Thee, even as a man talketh with his friend, and how Thou answerest by inward solace and holy thoughts ; I know that no true comfort or help can descend into my heart but by prayer, and I have numberless examples thereof in our Lord Jesus Christ, and in all the Saints; and yet, O Lord, how slow I am to pray, how apt to trust to my own efforts and wisdom, rather than to Thy help and grace. Oh forgive me for such foolish security, and contempt of Thy Divine promise. Remember not Thy threatening, that him who despiseth Thy grace Thou wilt despise; and that they who run after strange help shall have trouble of heart. Give me rather the spirit of aspiration and prayer; teach me to think of Thy blessed promises: 'Blessed is he who calleth on the name of the Lord.' 'The Lord is nigh unto all such as call upon Him.' 'Whatsoever ye ask the Father in my name, He will give it you.'

Ah! Lord, unto Whom all hearts are open, Who triest the hearts and the reins, Thou knowest how wavering are all human minds; Thou canst govern the vessel of my soul far better than I can. Arise, O Lord, and command the stormy wind and the troubled sea of my heart to be still, and at peace in Thee, that I may look up to Thee undisturbed, and abide in union with Thee, my Lord. Let me not be carried hither and thither by wandering thoughts; but, forgetting all else, let me see and hear Thee alone. Take away through Thy grace all that might hinder me in this work of prayer, whether it be this world with its fashion that passeth away, or the will of the flesh. Renew my spirit; sanctify my senses; kindle in me Thy Light, that it may shine within me, and my heart may burn in love and adoration towards Thee. Soften my heart to feel the flame of Thy Holy Spirit, to perceive His answer of love and inward consolation. May He sigh and pray and praise and give thanks in my soul, and bear witness with my spirit that I am Thy child. May He warm and kindle my cold heart with heavenly fire, and make intercession for me with groanings which cannot be uttered. Yea, let Thy Holy Spirit dwell in me continually, and make me Thy temple and sanctuary, and fill me with divine love and light and life, with devout and heavenly thoughts, with comfort and strength, with joy and peace. Unite me, O Father, through the same Spirit with Thy dear Son Jesus Christ, that I may pray in, and through, and with Him as my Head; and, as with Him, so may the Holy Spirit give me fellowship also with all faithful hearts and with the whole Church, that I may pray with and for and in Thy Church, as in Thy sanctuary;

and may be heard for the sake of our Lord Jesus Christ. Amen.

J. Arndt, 1555-1621.

III.

Praise to God.

BLESS the Lord, O my soul; and all that is in me praise His holy Name. Bless the Lord, O my soul; and forget not all His benefits.

Thee, Lord, I praise, whom all the angels and blessed spirits praise and worship: I would unite my voice to their songs. My soul soars above created things, and the eye of faith gazes upon Thee Who didst create them all. I forsake all lower thoughts, and seek to make my dwelling above, that I may behold Thee, the Sun of Righteousness, the Light of all rational beings. O that I might praise Thee with every faculty of my soul, Thou gracious God; that I might thank Thee worthily for every manifestation of Thy mercy; but Thy greatness, Thy goodness, and Almighty power cannot be expressed in my weak prayers. I can but desire to praise Thee, and to cleave to Thee with a mighty love. My God, my Life, my Strength, give enlightenment to my mind, and the fire of devotion to my heart; and let the words of my mouth be acceptable in Thy sight, O Father. Hallow my soul, and cleanse me from all stains of sin, that the pure sacrifice of my thanksgiving may be pleasing unto Thee. Lay hold upon my spirit, and make it a dwelling-place for Thyself, that I may know Thee, and worship Thee in spirit and in truth. Let Thy glory be ever in my mouth, for who is like unto Thee, O Lord, Thou Fountain of all goodness; and who can fully declare Thy Name? Unto Thee belong honour, thanks, and love, Who art our God from everlasting. Amen.

St. Augustine.

IV.

We love Him because He first loved us.

LATE have I loved Thee, O Thou Eternal Truth and Goodness: late have I sought Thee, my Father! But Thou didst seek me, and when Thou didst suffer Thyself to be found of me, when Thou shinedst forth upon me, then I knew Thee and learnt to love Thee. I thank Thee, O my Light, that Thou didst thus shine upon me; that Thou didst teach me what Thou wouldst be unto me, and what grace Thou hadst in store for me, Thy servant. For Thou didst say unto my soul, I am thy salvation; and didst incline Thy face in pity unto me, who am but dust and ashes. Therefore will I speak of Thy love, and praise Thy compassions.

Alas for the time when I knew Thee not! Alas for my blindness and deafness, when I saw Thee not, neither heard Thy voice! I was absorbed in the creature, but Thee, my Creator and my Father, I found not. But when Thy Light dawned upon me, I beheld Thee and I loved Thee. Oh that I had loved Thee sooner!

O Thou Whose name is Wonderful and Glorious, who is like unto Thee, or who has loved me as Thou hast done? Thee, the Creator of heaven and earth, Thee, the Eternal Ruler of all things, have I been brought to know as my Father in Jesus Christ. Thy mercy has been manifested unto me in Thy Eternal Son; my heart has tasted the refreshment of Thy consolations; and the powers of the life which is to come have descended upon my soul. Unto me came Thy Light and Thy Truth; unto me hath been granted an entrance into Thy kingdom. Thou hast forgiven my sins through faith in my Redeemer, and Thou hast deigned to fill my heart with joy in the Holy Ghost.

Thou, Lord, hast become my Hope, my Comfort, my Strength, my All! In Thee doth my soul rejoice. The darkness vanished from before mine eyes, and I beheld Thee, the Sun of Righteousness. When I loved darkness, I knew Thee not, but wandered on from night to night. But Thou didst lead me out of that blindness; Thou didst take me by the hand and call me to Thee, and now I can thank Thee, and Thy mighty voice which hath penetrated to my inmost heart.

O Thou holy and unspeakable, Thou wonderful and mighty God, Whose power and wisdom hath no end, before Whom all powers tremble, at Whose glance the heavens and the earth flee away, Thou art Love, Thou art my Father, and I will love and worship Thee for ever and ever!

Thou hast deigned to show pity on me, and a ray from Thy light hath shone upon mine inward eye. Guide me on into the perfect light, that it may illumine me wholly, and that all darkness may flee away. Let the holy flame of Thy love so burn in my heart that it be made pure, and I may see Thee, O God; for it is the pure in heart who see Thee. Thou hast set me free; Thou hast drawn me to Thee; therefore forsake me not, but keep me always in Thy grace. Guide me, and rule me, and perfect me for Thy kingdom. Amen.

St. Augustine.

V.

The Love of God in Christ Jesus.

INFINITE Love in Christ Jesus, Thou Well-spring of all sweetness, Thee do I now and ever seek; Thee do I call upon with the desire of my soul. Come Thou to meet me with Thy refreshing tenderness that I may hasten to Thee; for I cannot love nor receive Thee save by Thy grace, which must awaken me unto a new life. O set up Thy kingdom within me, with the righteousness of faith, with peace and joy in Thy love. Exercise me in daily repentance, that so my heart may ever return to Thee anew, whenever it has been led astray by quitting Thy side. Behold I bring Thee my will, unite it firmly with Thine own. Be Thou in Thy love sweeter to me than all the sweetness of the world. Instruct me by Thy Word and Spirit how to love Thee, and to obey Thee from warm affection. My thoughts must learn to turn most often and willingly to Thee; my lips to speak of Thee; my will gladly to forget what is merely temporal. O enter into my inmost heart; let a perpetual delight in heavenly things be awakened within me, like a fountain flowing unto eternal life. Let me never linger where Thou art not; and let me become anxious and fearful wherever I find Thee not. Help me in true love to Thee to accept the hostility of the world with joy, and never to be ashamed of Thee. May Thy love dispel all fear of man, and all unworthy desire to please; and give me a longing so to cleave to Thee, that neither height, nor depth, nor any other creature may separate me from Thee. Amen.

Neumann, 1700.

VI.

The Coming of our Lord Jesus Christ.

O LORD Jesus Christ, I bid Thee welcome, Who through Thy wondrous coming upon earth hast brought Thyself so near to us poor lost mortals, and hast offered us Thy eternal salvation. Every humble and hungering and believing soul now welcomes Thee with joy as her Lord; and my heart also would go forth to meet Thee. Enter in, Thou Blessed of Thy heavenly Father; stand not without at the door of my heart. Knock not in vain by Thy Word, but open that door unto Thyself. Awaken me from the sleep of careless indifference, of vanity and love of the flesh and the world; and let me cast no lingering look behind on my old sins. O Lord Jesus, Thou comest unto me so humble and meek, how can I help but love Thee? Thou art so lowly of heart, why should I be ashamed to show Thee all my wretchedness, and acknowledge the punishment I deserve? Thou art come to take away our sins. O make an end of the enmity which my sins have put between me and God, and reconcile me through repentance to Thy Father. Come into my heart, and bring the Spirit of grace and prayer to make intercession for me. Come and bestow on me Thy perfect redemption for the sake of which Thou art manifested in the flesh. Fulfil in me the aim of Thy advent; deliver my evil nature from the bonds of sin and vanity, and bring it under Thy gentle yoke. Govern my whole being as Thou wilt, unto the obedience of the truth. Art Thou not our King? O then rule over our will, that we may willingly and faithfully follow Thy gentle staff, and let Thy sceptre be a right sceptre over us. Dost Thou not come as a Teacher from God, to show us the true way?

O then shine into our souls as a clear Light, that we may follow Thee, the Light of Life, and go astray no more in the darkness of our blinded hearts. Wilt Thou not come, O Immanuel, as our Mediator and Intercessor? Oh come; it is time that we be made free from an evil conscience, and receive power to draw near with joy to the Father through faith and prayer in Thy name. Therefore come, O Thou our Righteousness, and humble our proud nature to repentance and contrition. Come, Thou our Wisdom, rescue us from our own foolishness, and teach us to know Thee and Thy Father with a living knowledge. Come, Thou our Sanctification; let us cleave no longer to the mire of vain pleasures and earthly desires; but wash, and purify, and sanctify us in Thy name through the Spirit of Holiness. Come, O Redeemer, and redeem us from all evil that now vexes and torments us. Come, Thou truest Friend, enter into our desolate hearts; go in unto Thy temple, drive out thence all unholy thoughts and impulses, and bring in with Thee Thy own tender love, Thy deep humility, Thy untiring patience, Thy gentleness and meekness, Thy submission to the Father, Thy separatedness from the world. Thus make Thou of me a man after Thine own heart, and show forth the mighty power of Thy salvation, how Thou canst tread Thy foes under foot. O Lord, if Thou wilt thus take up Thy abode in my heart, then sin and death, the world and the devil, must give place unto Thee, and nothing can hold me in bondage any more. Therefore come unto me quickly in all Thy power. Lo! my heart is open unto Thee; take full possession of it; use me as Thou wilt; let me never resist Thee more.

Come thus unto me with Thy gracious presence now, and so shall I not be dismayed when Thou shalt come again unto judgment, but shall lift up my head with joy, and haste to meet Thee. My spirit saith Come! and Thou answerest graciously, Lo! I come quickly. Amen, even so come Lord Jesus, at every moment of this earthly life, and abide with me for ever and ever. Amen.

Gottfried Arnold, 1697.

VII.

The Incarnation of our Lord.

O THOU most loving and gracious Son of God, Jesus Christ, Thou true Lover of the human race, unto Thee be praise and thanks for ever, for Thy blessed

Incarnation and birth, for Thy great love and mercy in taking upon Thee our flesh and blood, and becoming our Brother, and thus exalting us to be sons and heirs with Thee!

Thou mighty King and Lord of lords, Whose power and glory and riches have no end, how hast Thou bowed Thyself to our poor, low, weak human nature! How hast Thou glorified that nature by raising it, in the unity of Thy Divine Person, to the right hand of Thy heavenly Father! Thou hast taken a human body and soul on Thee that Thou mightest help us both in body and soul. Human nature was wholly corrupted by sin, but in Thee is it restored to perfect purity and holiness. It was accursed, but in Thee is it most blessed, O Thou Blessed of the Lord, in Whom all the nations of the earth are blessed. It was under the wrath of God, but how hath He loved it in Thee! It was separated from Him, but how closely hast Thou united it to Him once more! Who then shall lay aught to our charge? Who can be against us? For God hath made an eternal covenant with us in the incarnation of His dear Son; a covenant of everlasting friendship and love, a real atonement, and a union whereby we have a sonship, a brotherhood, and a peace that cannot be taken away.

That we might live, hath the Life itself come down to us. That we might have light, hath the Light itself shined into our darkness. That we might have comfort in our misery, hath the Fount of all comfort streamed from Heaven into this dark region of sorrow. That we might become the children of God, hath the Son of God become man. Oh how delightful is Thy presence and Thy fellowship! How sweet are Thy words, Thou Fairest among the sons of men! Oh, my Friend, enter into my heart; my Brother, despise me not; Thou Lover of my soul, forsake me nevermore!

He Whom I love hath been made man, hath been crucified, hath died for me, that His life and death might alike assure me of His love; that I might be made one with Him, and live and die in His fellowship, and have the calmness, the peace, the hope, the safety, the eternal blessedness, which He only can bestow. Amen.

J. Arndt, 1555–1621.

VIII.

On the Presentation in the Temple.

BLESSED Lord Jesus, Who in the days of Thy flesh didst voluntarily submit to the law, that Thou mightest redeem them that were under the law, and that we might receive the adoption of children; grant that even as Thou wert presented by Thy dear mother, Mary, in the Temple of the Lord, so I, after the cleansing of my sins, may present myself to my God, and offer my body as a living sacrifice, holy and acceptable to the Lord. Let me with the aged Simeon serve Thee only day by day, in piety and godly fear; that Thy good and Holy Spirit may be in me and abide with me. Let me receive Thee to my heart by faith, as Simeon clasped Thee in his arms; that so I too may at last close my life with joy, and say with him, in perfect trust, 'Lord, now lettest Thou Thy servant depart in peace, according to Thy will. For mine eyes have seen Thy Salvation, which Thou hast prepared before the face of all people, to be a Light to lighten the Gentiles, and to be the Glory of Thy people Israel.' And then do Thou also receive my soul into Thine arms, and bear me safely into Thy glory. Amen.

Quirsfeld, 1642–1686.

IX.

Christ's Life our Pattern.

O GENTLE and loving Lord Jesu Christ, what a fair example of a holy and virtuous life hast Thou left us, that we should follow in Thy footsteps. Thou art the stainless mirror of all virtues, the perfect pattern of holiness, the blameless rule of piety, the unswerving standard of righteousness. Ah! how unlike is my sinful life to Thy holy one! I ought to live to Thee as a new creature, and I live far more in the old creature, more in Adam, than in my dear Lord Jesus Christ. I ought to live after the Spirit, yet I live after the flesh, though I well know that the Scripture says, 'If ye live after the flesh, ye shall die.' O thou gentle, patient, long-suffering Heart, forgive me my sin; cover my faults; cast me not away from Thy countenance; shut not Thy door against me as one unclean.

Weed out pride from my heart, the tares sown by the enemy, and plant within me Thy humility, which is the very root of all virtue. Take away thoroughly all spirit of grudging and revenge, and give me Thy generous meekness.

O Thou, the highest Beauty of Holiness, adorn my heart with pure faith, glowing love, and lively hope, with holy adoration and childlike awe! O Thou, my sole Trust, my Lover and my Hope, my Boast and my Glory, Thy life was nothing else but love, meekness, and humility; suffer then that noble life to dwell in me, that virtuous life to be also mine. Make me a member of Thy Body, and of one Spirit with Thyself, that Thou mayst live in me and I in Thee, and I may live unto Thee not unto myself. Grant that I may so know and love Thee that I may walk even as Thou hast walked. Thou art the Eternal Way, and Truth, and Life; then guide and instruct and quicken me. Make me Thy instrument that all my members and powers of body and soul may be hallowed to Thy use, not yielded to the Evil One to work his evil will of pride deceit, anger, covetousness, or impurity in me. For these are his image, from which Thou, O Fairest and Perfect Image of our God, wilt deliver me. Impart unto me somewhat of Thy beauty. Renew me inwardly and outwardly according to Thine own likeness, till this life is accomplished. Let me die to the world, that I may live to Thee. Let me arise with Thee, that with Thee I may ascend unto Heaven.

Let me be crucified with Thee, that I may also enter into Thy glory. Amen.

J. Arndt, 1555–1621.

X.

At the beginning of the Week before Easter.

(CALLED IN GERMANY THE WEEK OF STILLNESS.)

LORD Jesus Christ, Lamb of God, who takest away the sins of the world, give us Thy peace.

Praise waiteth for Thee, O God, in the stillness of Zion; grant that Thy gentle and holy Spirit may now make my soul wait in stillness upon Thee. I praise Thee for Thy unfailing compassion, in which Thou hast suffered me once more to reach the beginning of this great Week of Stillness, wherein Thou didst give the only-begotten Son of Thy love to such countless pains and sorrows, even unto the death of the Cross, for the whole world, and therefore for me too, a sinner. Now indeed, at this great season must I magnify anew the eternal redemption which hath been won for me by my Lord Jesus Christ. Ah! Lord, would that all men everywhere, at home and abroad, by day and by night, might wait in tranquil silence before Thee this week, Who now, having conquered the pains of death, art crowned with glory and honour, and sittest at the right hand of God in His holy Temple. But above all, still Thou the restlessness of this unquiet heart of mine, O Lord of Peace; wean it from its many distractions by that same Spirit wherein Thou hast offered Thyself unto the Father, that so it may listen with attentive ears to Thy voice, when Thou speakest within me, saying, 'Thou hast made Me to toil with thy sins, thou hast wearied Me with thine iniquities, yet I, even I, am He that blotteth thy transgressions for mine own sake, and will not remember thy sins.' Yes, when Thy heavenly appeal is heard, 'Think upon Me, O Jacob; and forget Me not, O house of Israel,' may the response come from the depths of a renewed heart: I do meditate upon Thee, O blessed Lord, and will ever be thankful unto Thee afresh. I will strive not to make a wrong use of Thy sufferings and death, but to contemplate them with earnest reverence. I desire to be made obedient unto Thy Cross, that I may be able to say with truth, I am crucified with Christ, I am dead with Him that I may live unto God; henceforth it is not I but Christ that liveth in me. Thy first entrance into this world, Thy whole walk in poverty, obedience, and lowliness, lay a sufficient obligation on me to become Thy property; but since Thou willingly enduredst such unnumbered woes even unto Thy death for our sake, Thou hast so bound me unto Thee, that if I could forget or deny Thee, it were just indeed that Thou shouldst forget and deny me before God and His holy angels. Bless, then, O merciful Saviour, Thy Passion in its beginning, continuance, and end unto my soul. May its beginning be the beginning of primitive and entire trust in Thy Name, with a sincere heart. May its continuance guide me more deeply into the knowledge of the mystery of Thy Cross, ground me in love, impart a willing surrender to the fellowship of Thy death. May its end work in me patience and hope, that I may abide still before Thee amid all outward contradictions, may submit to Thy will simply in every circumstance of my lot, and so endure through weal and woe unto the end, that I may ever rejoice with Thee in Thy glory. Amen.

Storr, 1756.

XI.

The Consolation of Passion Week.

THOUGH I am a miserable sinner, and my many misdeeds torment my conscience, and often make me fearful, yet am I filled with contentment and joy when I gaze upon Thy wounded Form, so full of mercy and grace, for there I behold how very gentle and loving Thou art towards all weary and heavy-laden hearts; how willing Thou art to refresh and quicken them; how inexhaustible is Thy compassion. He who desires much shall find much, more than even he has asked or hoped. In this confidence do I come to Thee, O Lord Christ, and ask for great mercy, for my sins are great; heal me, O Lord Christ, and cleanse me from all evil by Thy precious blood.

Let Thy grace transcend my transgression; seek me in Thy pity as a lost sheep of Thine, bear me upon Thy shoulders, and bring me back into the right way. Lead me and guide me, for the sake of the merits of Thy Cross and Passion, even unto eternal life. Amen.

Musculus, 1514-1581.

XII.

For the Thursday before Easter.

LORD Jesus Christ, Who with Thy own sacred lips dost say, that if he that is hungry and athirst cometh unto Thee, Thou wilt so feed him and give him to drink, that he shall never hunger nor thirst any more—Ah! Lord, here cometh unto Thee a poor soul, hungering and thirsting for the food and drink of eternal righteousness and bliss. O Thou Bread of Life, feed me who hunger, with Thy true Body! O Thou Well of Life, quicken and refresh me who thirst, with Thy Blood, that, satisfied and strengthened, I may arise from this dark valley unto Thee in heaven, where Thou sittest on the right hand of Thy heavenly Father, and dost plead for us; where, free from all thirst and hunger, I shall praise Thee in eternal joy and gladness, with Thy Father and the Holy Spirit, world without end. Amen.

St. Augustine.

XIII.

Gethsemane.

LORD Jesus, fix my eyes now and ever on those inward sorrows of heart which Thou hast borne for our sins with such inexpressible anguish in the garden of Gethsemane. Let the great drops of blood which fell from Thee there so deeply impress my soul with Thy boundless love, that the impression may continue with me through life, and give me all needful strength at my last hour to be faithful to Thee unto death. Unite me to Thyself in faith, blend my will with Thine, that I may offer myself in Thee to Thy heavenly Father, and willingly embrace the fellowship of Thy sufferings, and bow to whatsoever may be appointed for me. Let Thy blood, O Lord, penetrate me to the washing away the stains of sin in body and soul. As Thou didst worship Thy Father in all humility upon Thy knees, so may Thy Spirit cast me down from my pride and self-will unto the dust at Thy feet. May I so yield myself to Thee that not my will but Thine be done in me. Help me to watch and pray that I fall not into temptation; and arouse me afresh whenever, like Thy disciples, I sink into false security. Make my spirit willing, though the flesh be weak. And when in any hour of trial or of death, the sweat of anguish stands upon my brow, keep me not the less true to the last. O faithful Saviour, be with me in all conflicts, even as the angel strengthened Thee in Thy weakness. Plead for me, O great High-priest, Who didst offer Thyself with strong crying and tears, for Thou art ever merciful and hast pity on my infirmity, for Thou wast also tempted even as we are, yet without sin. Help me then by the memory of Thy sorrows in all trial present or to come; and if I weary and slumber in the strife, awaken and warn me that I fall not under temptation, but may be made more than a conqueror in Thee. Amen.

G. Arnold, 1697.

XIV.

For Good Friday.

AH! Lord, Thou eternal and merciful God and Father, look down on Thy dear Son, and behold what great anguish He must needs suffer for my sake. Ah! Father, see Who suffers it, and behold with

Thy mercy him for whom it is borne. Is it not, O most faithful Father, Thy Son, the guiltless Lamb of God, Whom Thou hast given to suffer for a servant? Is it not the Lord of Life and Glory, Who is led as a lamb to the slaughter, and hath been obedient unto death, yea, hath taken the most shameful death upon Himself? Ah! think, O God Who desirest the life of the world, it is Thy only and beloved Son, the Begotten of Thy heart, Whom Thou hast made partaker of my weakness. Yes, of a truth, it is Thy Godhead Who hath taken my nature upon Him, and hath suffered Himself to be nailed upon the cross, and hath borne the heavy punishment of our sins. Ah! Lord, turn Thine eyes upon this great work of Thy mercy and goodness. Look on Thy dear Son, how His whole body is stretched out upon the cross. Look at His hands, whence the blood is welling as from a spring, and forgive me graciously all the misdeeds that my hands have committed. Look, O Lord, upon His pierced side, and quicken me with the blood that floweth thence. Look at His feet, which have never trod the paths of sin but have ever walked according to Thy laws, how they are pierced with nails, and vouchsafe me grace, that my feet may keep Thy ways; take away from me the way of wickedness, and let me evermore walk in Thy paths. Amen.

St. Augustine.

XV.

At the Tomb.

LORD Jesu Christ, at the opening of this Week of Stillness, I prayed to Thee for a quiet, undistracted heart; now beside Thy grave I pray, Give me grace to make my whole soul calm and still. Thy death upon the Cross brought stillness alike upon Thy friends and foes who before were in wild commotion. All felt Thy power in Thy death, Thou Strength of the Most High. Thy foes are startled and dismayed; the restless populace is dispersed; Thy mother, whose soul has been pierced with a sharp sword, and Thy disciples, wait in stillness through the Sabbath, according to the law. Now sanctify to me the day of Thy death and burial as a time of holy stillness. If the preaching of Thy Cross which I have heard this week hath entered my heart and seized my mind, and disquieted it with wholesome thoughts of my own guilt, let me now in this evening hour rest peacefully on the grace which Thy sorrows have won for me. Suffer not, O Lord, the treasures of salvation which lie hidden in the mystery of the Cross to have been once more displayed to me so richly in vain; but let me in the quiet spirit of faith lay hold upon them, that my heart may be fired with ardent love to Thee, and my conduct may be moulded to follow the pattern that Thou hast set before us. So shall this renewed contemplation of Thy suffering be blest to me for time and eternity. Amen.

Starr, 1756.

XVI.

The Risen and Ascended Saviour.

O JESU, our Lord and King, Who art highly exalted, in what glory has Thy course ended, how have the heavenly hosts welcomed Thee when Thou didst enter Thy kingdom as Conqueror over Sin, Death, and Hell, and didst sit down on the right hand of God!

Ah! we strangers here below on earth desire to partake in the joy of the heavenly ones, to bow the knee and give glory to Thee with them. Hosanna to the Son of David! Hosanna in the highest! Rule, O Jesus! send forth the sceptre out of Zion, and bring all hearts under

Thy sway. Thou hast passed into heaven, but we are yet dwelling on earth; Thou hast completed Thy course, but we are yet treading the narrow and thorny way. Help us, and let all our steps be sanctified for the sake of Thy sorrowful path; may all Thy deeds, Thy self-denial, Thy prayers, Thy sufferings, hallow ours. Hold us by Thy strengthening hand, that we may walk fearlessly forward on the way that leads to heaven, not fainting beneath its toils, not standing still as beginners, but going on through Thy Spirit to holiness, perfection, and the final bliss. And to this end, teach us the practice of true earnest prayer from the heart, of quiet retirement, of patient waiting for Thy Spirit from on high. Jesu Christ, Thou our Head art glorified, and we are Thy members. Thou hast said, 'When I am lifted up, I will draw all men unto Me.' Draw us then out of all our wickedness, our selfishness, our absorption in the things of sense and sight, into Thine own heavenly life, that we may live with Thee where now Thou art. Let all worldliness be banished out of us, that we may not lose ourselves in what is temporal, but seek after that which is eternal; so shall we, with full hearts and true love, cleave to Thee alone, and occupy ourselves with that which alone can comfort and sustain us in the hour of trial or of death.

O Prince of Life, teach us to stand more boldly on Thy side, to face the world and all our adversaries more courageously, and not to let ourselves be dismayed by any storm of temptation ; may our eyes be steadfastly fixed on Thee in fearless faith ; may we trust Thee with perfect confidence that Thou wilt keep us, save us, and bring us through by the power of Thy grace and the riches of Thy mercy. Come and set up Thy kingdom in our hearts ; unto Thee we submit ourselves and our powers, heart and mind, senses and thought—all must be subject to Thee, all Thy faithful people must learn to be guided by the tokens of Thy good pleasure, and walk as ever in Thy sight.

And O mighty King, bring under Thy sway all who as yet rebel against Thee. Send out apostles and teachers who shall make known to sinners the greatness of Thy majesty and the greatness of Thy love, that Thy kingdom may be spread abroad even unto the ends of the world. Ah ! when, O Lord, wilt Thou come in Thy power that the hearts of all nations may be turned unto Thee !

Awaken us from all indolence and dreaminess ; teach us to walk before Thee with burning lamps, with cheerful hearts, day by day expecting our summons home, that when it comes, we may be found ready. Give us abundantly the oil of Thy Spirit and Thy Love, that we may be kept alert in constant watchfulness and unwearied prayer. Draw us heavenwards, that we may every day mount thither in faith, till we do so perfectly on that day when Thou dost call us home.

Bless all Thy children throughout the earth; mould them to Thy heavenly image, so that their holy conduct may draw many to Thee and make them willing subjects of Thy rule. Strengthen all, strengthen each one, to be faithful to Thee unto the end.

O Lord, we lay our sighs upon Thy heart; bring them, O Priest in the Holy of holies, bring our prayers unto Thy Father, obtain a gracious hearing, seal Thy Word in our hearts, and fulfil all our desires. Amen.

Tersteegen, 1731.

XVII.

On the Coming of the Holy Spirit.

LORD God, the Holy Ghost, Almighty Comforter, Thou who art the flame of love in the unity of the Godhead, and the holy fellowship of the Almighty Father and

His beloved Son; Thou precious Comforter of the sorrowful, descend with Thy glorious power into my heart, take possession of it, abide in it, rule and guide it unto all goodness. Gladden, O Lord, this dark and defiled dwelling with the shining of Thy light; water it with Thy springs, and quicken it with Thy strength, for it is dry and parched.

Touch, O God, the very hidden centre of the inner man with Thy life-giving ardour, for it is slothful and careless; penetrate it with the fire of Thy holy love, and burn out the inmost evil of the lust of the flesh; water me from the fountain of Thy joys, that I may thirst no more for the passing pleasures of the world. Judge me, O God, and plead my cause against an ungodly nation. Teach me to do according to Thy good pleasure, for Thou art my God. I believe and know, that in whatsoever man Thou dwellest Thou dost make him the abode of God the Father and the Son. O, well for him with whom Thou art a guest, for through Thee will the Father and the Son make their abode with him; through Thee we may come boldly before the face of God and pray. Come now, O merciful Comforter of the sad in heart; come and teach us to pray aright and to obey our Heavenly Father; come and be our Defence in time of need, our help in the day of trial; come and cleanse us from our sins, and heal our wounds. Come and strengthen the weak, and raise up the prisoners; come and teach the ignorant, govern the humble and the contrite, and scatter the proud in the imagination of their hearts. Come, O Thou merciful Father of all orphans, Thou kind Judge of the widow, be Thou the confidence of the poor, and the solace of the sick. Come and lead aright those who are gone astray, and deliver the wretched out of their troubles. Come and adorn us with thy precious gifts, and be our comfort and hope in death. Come, O God the Holy Ghost, and have mercy upon us!

Dispose my heart towards Thee, and incline Thyself graciously unto me, that I may place an unshaken trust in Thy Word, and listen to it with due reverence, and lay it up heedfully in my heart. Despise me not for my weakness, but strengthen my faith according to Thy great mercy, through Jesus Christ my Saviour, who liveth and reigneth with the Father in the unity of the Spirit, one God evermore. Amen.

St. Augustine.

XVIII.

Before the Holy Communion.

BEHOLD, O my God, I am the man who went down to Jericho and fell among thieves; sorely have they wounded me, and left me lying half-dead; come, Lord, Thou faithful Helper, raise me up and heal me.

I have sinned heavily in my whole conduct, and done evil in Thy sight. I have not exercised myself in the knowledge of Thee; I have been unthankful for Thy many benefits, and have not praised Thy name aright. Often and in many ways have I abstained from uttering Thy truths; and when Thou hast stood and knocked at the door of my heart, I have been slothful and have not welcomed Thee as I ought. This body, which fadeth like a shadow and shall be the food of worms, I have cherished too much; I have defiled my lips with unseemly words, and have been negligent and careless about Thy wholesome Word; I have not ever and always turned away my eyes from beholding vanity, nor kept my ears from listening to unprofitable things; many a time my hands have not served my neighbour in his need, while my feet were swift to evil. What need I say more, my God?

From the crown of my head to the sole of my feet there is no health in me.

Ah! my Lord Jesus, hadst Thou not died for me on the Cross and redeemed me, my soul must have perished for ever in hell; but now am I a partaker, O merciful Lord! in Thy great salvation. O reject not one, my Saviour, whom Thou hast so dearly purchased with Thy precious blood. Behold I am a wandering sheep; seek me, Thou good Shepherd, and bear me home to Thy fold according to Thy promise. Thou hast promised, O my Helper! that whensoever a poor sinner shall sigh unto Thee, Thou wilt hearken unto him. Now see how heartily I mourn and acknowledge my sins, which are ever before me. In truth I am not worthy to be called Thy son, yet make me, my Saviour, to hear of joy and gladness, and turn not away Thy face from me.

O Thou Son of the Living God, Only Begotten of Thy Father before all worlds! blessed are those who love Thee, and desire nought else; blessed are those who daily remember Thee, and worthily feed upon Thee; blessed are those who abide in Thee and keep Thy ways unto their life's end! O Holy Bread of Heaven, how rich and bounteous art Thou; how overflowing are Thy gifts! For Thou excludest no man, unless it be that he despises Thee, and refuses to come to Thee. Is any one young and small, let him come boldly to Thee and eat, and he will grow and increase: he will put away his childish mind and walk in the paths of true wisdom. Is any yet weak, let him hasten to Thee and eat, and he shall soon wax strong. Is any sick, he shall be relieved. Is any dead in sins, let him but hearken to Thee and he shall attain everlasting life. And though one be strong and full-grown, yet will he perceive that he is still in need of many things, and in Thee will he find abundantly that whereby he may daily increase in them. None can live a moment without Thee, for it is Thou alone who givest life to all creatures. O God, the joy and consolation of my heart, my soul is glad in Thee, and my spirit hath a desire unto Thee; for all who turn away from Thee must pine for ever. O Thou true and invisible Light which never can be quenched, behold me sitting like a poor blind man beside the way, and crying unto Thee: 'Jesus, Thou Son of David, have mercy upon me; open the eyes of my soul that I may see Thee!' Lord, be merciful to me a sinner! Thou art my Help and my Confidence, oh help me unto eternal salvation! Lord, my Physician, heal me. I am naked and suffer cold, O Thou rich Lord, cover me with the mantle of Thy righteousness. My soul hungers in this desert, do Thou, Lord, the true Food, quicken my heart. My soul is athirst: Lord, Thou art the true healing Spring, water and refresh my spirit with Thy wholesome comfort. I am come into the deep mire, and my strength faileth me; I am far out on the seas, and the floods threaten to swallow me up; I have cried till I am weary and hoarse, and the waters of death are coming into my very soul. Save me, O Lord, my Shield, my Deliverer, my Comfort, my Refuge, my Strength, my King, and my God, for Thy mercies' sake! Amen.

St. Jerome.

XIX.

The Holy Communion.

I.

LORD Jesus Christ, the true Shepherd and Bishop of my soul, Who hast said: 'I am the Bread of Life; he who eateth of Me shall never hunger, and he who believeth in Me shall never thirst;' I come to Thee and humbly entreat that Thou wouldst prepare me through true faith to be a fit guest at Thy heavenly supper. To-day wilt Thou feed me, Thy poor sheep, in green pastures, and lead me to the fresh water of life. Thou wilt restore my soul, and lead me in the straight path for Thy Name's sake. Thou wilt make me worthy to sit at Thy table, and wilt fill for me the cup of Thy love and grace. Lo! I come as Thy sheep to Thy pasture, to the Bread of Heaven, the Spring of Life; O Thou true and precious Bread, awaken in me spiritual hunger, a holy thirst, that I may pant after Thee as the hart after the waterbrooks.

And above all, give me real contrition for my sins; put on me the true marriage-garment of faith, whereby I may lay hold on Thy holy merits and cling thereto, that I be not an unworthy guest. And give me also a humble, placable disposition, that I may forgive my enemies from the bottom of my heart; take away all the root of bitterness and animosity, and plant love and pity in my soul instead, that I may love my neighbour, yea, all men in Thee. Under the old covenant the manna was preserved in a golden vessel for a memorial. Ah! would to God, that I might so keep Thee in the shrine of a pure heart. Ah, Lord! Thou hast said Thyself, 'the whole need not a physician, but the sick.' I am sick, I have need of Thee as the heavenly Physician of my soul. Thou hast said: 'Come unto Me, all ye that are weary and heavy laden, and I will refresh you.'

See, Lord! I come heavy-laden with many sins, take them from me, relieve me from this great burden. I come as one unclean, oh! purify me; as blind, give me light; as poor, make me inwardly rich; as lost, seek me out; as condemned, save me. O Jesu! truest Friend of my soul, lead me away from myself unto Thyself, yea into Thee; for in Thee I live, and in myself am dead; in Thee am I justified, and in myself wholly sinful; in Thee am I saved, in myself am I full of condemnation. In Thee have I full satisfaction, Thou art my All. Abide then in me, and let me ever abide in Thee; as Thou hast said, he who eateth My flesh, and drinketh My blood, shall abide in Me and I in him, and I will raise him up at the last day. Amen.

J. Arndt, 1555–1621.

2.

I THANK Thee, O Blessed Lord Jesu Christ, for Thy unspeakable love in redeeming the human race by Thy precious death; and pray Thee humbly that Thou suffer not Thy blood to have been shed in vain for me, a poor sinner, but wouldest feed my soul with Thy body, and quicken my spirit with Thy blood, that I may grow continually in the knowledge of Thee, in Thy fear and love, and in Christian conduct; and may abide a true member of Thy Body and Thy holy Church. Amen.

St. Augustine.

3.

O LORD Jesu Christ, though of a truth I am not worthy that Thou shouldest come under my roof, yet am I in sore need of Thy help, and desirous of Thy grace, that I may attain godliness and salvation. I come now in no other confidence than this, that I have heard the sweet words wherewith Thou invitest me to Thy table, and dost promise me, unworthy though I be, forgiveness of my sins through Thy body and blood, which I eat and drink in this Sacrament. O dear Lord, I know that Thy Divine word and promise are true; I doubt them not; and, resting on them, I eat and drink with Thee. Be it unto me according to Thy word. Amen.

Luther.

4.

O THOU mighty Grace of God! I an unworthy and sinful man come unto Thee at Thy bidding and command, for Thou hast promised us sinners that Thou wilt refresh us. Be it unto me according to Thy promise, even as Thou wilt; to Thee I offer myself here, wholly and entirely. Do with me, poor worthless creature as I am, according to Thy mercy; I would be Thine for ever, break down my self-will, and rule me by Thy will; I have nought in myself; I throw myself utterly upon Thy grace. Amen.

Jacob Böhme, 1575-1624.

5.

O THOU King and Saviour, most worthy of all praise, Lord Jesu Christ, to-day at the Holy Feast hast Thou condescended infinitely unto me, and hast mysteriously, but essentially, imparted Thyself to me under the bread and wine. Thus hast Thou shown me such extraordinary grace, that Thou hast united me to Thyself in righteousness and judgment, in love and mercy; nay, Thou hast betrothed me to Thyself, though but weak was the faith with which I came to Thee.

I can do nought in return but offer myself wholly unto Thee as a living sacrifice, which was done long ago in my baptism, which I did with many tears when I first partook of Thy

Holy Supper, which I have repeated many times since then at Thy altar, when I have made a lasting covenant with Thee, and have sworn to give Thee my trust, allegiance, and love, and to renounce Thy enemies and mine. This I do once more now, on this day of reconciliation and spiritual marriage, in the most solemn manner, and with the most sincere and earnest intention. I am Thine own, bought with a price, that I should live no more unto myself. If I live I live unto the Lord, and if I die, I die unto the Lord; therefore, living or dying, in soul and body, I am the Lord's.

Here then I renounce the vain world, and all that is of the world; all sensual delights, however alluring and excusable they may seem; the lust of the eye, and whatsoever promotes it; all pride and haughtiness of thought or manner. I renounce our enemy, Satan, and all his works; I will daily resist him, and, through the cross of Jesus, I will overcome him. I will watch the more carefully, the more craftily and secretly he plots my destruction. I renounce my own old nature with its perverted impulses wholly and entirely. The more this inner foe torments me, the more incessantly I have to battle with him, the more will I cry to my Saviour, and through the power of His death crucify the old Adam with all evil desires and lusts.

And on the other hand, I give myself with a willing heart and without reserve unto Christ as my rightful Lord, to be a living sacrifice unto Him, solely under His rule and guidance. Thee will I everywhere seek, and where Thou art not, there will I not be. When I go to my rest I will seek Thee and fall asleep in Thy bosom. When I awake I will instantly think of Thee, Thou Sun of Righteousness and long for Thy Light. When I am at work I will entreat Thy presence to bless my labour; when I eat Thou shalt be my Guest; when I am in company, I will bear in mind Thy presence, and gladly speak of Thee; when I am in solitude I will commune with Thee, and thus ever abide in Thee.

Of a truth Thou faithful Saviour shalt be all, all to me. It may be that I might for a time find pleasure apart from Thee; it may be that my blessed intercourse with Thee, my zeal in serving and following Thee, may bring upon me outward trials, difficulties, and enemies; yet will I not forsake Thee; yet will I count all pleasures, comfort, honour, and credit among men, which are contrary to Thee, as mere loss.

Thou, O God, shalt be the joy of my heart and my portion for ever.

My infinite Benefactor, in order that I may love Thee more practically, let me be henceforth a friend unto all men; whether they are kindly disposed to me or not; however insignificant they may seem; whether they are pious and members of Thee, or worldly in heart and untrue to Thee. Help me to feel an active love towards them all, according to my ability and opportunity. Let the unequalled love which Thou hast shown us in Thy life and sorrows, and taught us in Thy word, be my pattern and my incitement. And so I lay down at Thy feet all envy, pride, avarice, all coldness and hardness, all secret grudges, my sullen, irritable, passionate behaviour towards my fellow-creatures, and especially all falsehood and disguise. No one shall be judged, hurt, ridiculed, vexed, hated by me.

Yes, I will no more condemn hastily, or speak evil of my neighbour. I will bear not only with my enemies and slanderers, but with the weak, the eccentric, the impatient, and the passionate. I will look beyond their faults unto Thee, O Lord Jesu! on Thy Cross, where Thou didst pray so lovingly for Thy murderers, and bear so gently with their mockery. I will not turn away from the poor, but regard them as Thy brethren and mine; I will comfort, advise, and assist the widows and fatherless; I will pray often and heartily for all men, and especially for all Thy Christian servants. I will diligently endeavour to keep in the fellowship of the faithful who are scattered throughout the earth; and may those who love Thee and know Thy testimony admit me among their number. Daily would I grow firmer in faith, more humble, pure, tranquil and watchful, holy, and like Thee my Saviour. Ever will I seek first the kingdom of God and His righteousness, and next will I endeavour to perform the duties of my calling here, faithfully and conscientiously. I would live in the world but not be of the world; I would banish all deluding self-love; I would acknowledge my sins, trust in Thee, live and die unto Thee, and serve Thee for ever and ever. Amen.

W. G. Reiz, 1750.

XX.

Intercession for the Church.

O GOD and Father, since Thou hast brought me with a holy calling to the community of Thy elect servants in Thy Church on earth, so that I am united with them, and they with me, through Thy Spirit, in faith, love, and hope in our Lord Jesus Christ, I pray to Thee earnestly to bless and keep all my brethren and sisters in all places. Defend, sanctify, comfort, and provide for them, and preserve them by Thy power unto eternal life. Unto Thee, the All-knowing, their condition, their wants and dangers lie open; help all and each one of them, when and how they most need and desire Thy help. Console the sad, strengthen the weak, raise up the fallen, bring the lost and wandering back, and sanctify them by Thy truth. Be the comfort, the refreshment, the physician of the sick; feed the poor and destitute, defend the widow and the orphan; be the refuge of all fugitives, who are persecuted for Thy Name and truth's sake, who have to suffer oppression or captivity. Convert the sinful and the godless, release their souls from the snares of Satan, open their eyes to their own miserable condition, and bid them turn to Thee with their whole hearts. Preserve them by Thy mercy and long-suffering from utter ruin. Bring also the unbelievers throughout the world, Jews, Mahometans, and heathen, unto the knowledge of Thy dear Son Jesus Christ; and have mercy on all men.

Provide us and all congregations with godly,

enlightened and faithful teachers and pastors; arm them with gifts and power from heaven; bless their labours; and let the souls entrusted to their care prosper in sound instruction, living faith, strong consolation, and holiness of life. Give them boldness and joyfulness, and may they adorn their sacred office by holy and blameless conduct, and bring blessing on themselves and all who hear them by Thy Word and Spirit.

Give us in all places fatherly and conscientious rulers, men who love justice and peace; bestow on them the spirit of wisdom, good counsel, firmness, and the fear of Thee. Bless their government, and direct it to the honour of Thy Name, the protection and assistance of Thy Church, and the temporal and eternal welfare of all good subjects. And, in our own dear country and throughout Christendom, give and maintain to us blessed Peace, that we may pass our lives in rest and quiet, in righteousness and godliness.

Keep me and mine in faith, hope, and love; and suffer us not to fall into any deadly error, nor to be immersed in the godless indifference of these latter days. Teach us to long for Thy appearing; make Thou soon an end of all sin, and shame, and misery upon earth; deliver us from all evil, and bring us to Thine everlasting kingdom, so shall we see and praise Thee for ever. Amen.

Scriver, 1629-1693.

XXI.

Prayer for the Church.

O MERCIFUL GOD, Thou Father in Jesus Christ, I praise Thee for having called me to Thy invisible Church, and made me a living member in the spiritual Body of Christ. What would all earthly wealth avail me, if I had not the undying treasures which may one day accompany me into heaven? What avails honour in this world if I were not a child of Thy family, an heir of Thy heaven? And what am I, Lord, that Thou shouldst have brought me hither? In me was no strength or worthiness that Thou shouldst desire me. It is of Thy free grace that I have been born in the bosom of Thy Church, where I hear Thy precious Word preached, am refreshed with heavenly gifts in Christ, and am permitted to serve Thee in spirit and truth. For all this I have to thank Thy mercy, and through it alone I am what I am. Thou, O

Searcher of hearts, knowest who are Thine own, who will recognise and love each other more perfectly in heaven. Oh, hear my prayer when I pray for *all* who serve Thee in sincerity. Bless Thine heritage, and show Thyself an Almighty protector of all faithful hearts who know Thy Name.

Remember, O Lord, Thy covenant and Thy gracious promise, that Thou wilt never forget Thine own, for Thou hast graven them on Thy heart. Oh, let them be united in love as one heart and one soul. Let them love Thy Word, and encourage each other to good works, that their light may shine before men, and Thou mayest be glorified. Strengthen all our brethren who dwell amid the enemies of the truth; let no craft nor trial make them swerve aside; protect them from their enemies; comfort them in sadness; help them under oppression, that they may remain steadfast in faith, godly in life, patient in affliction, and unvanquished even in death.

Bring soon, O Lord, that glorious time when children shall be born to Thy Zion like the dew of the morning. Let the fulness of the heathen be gathered in, and Israel be saved; that Thy Name may be praised from the rising of the sun to the going down of the same, and all the world may have one fold and one Shepherd. And when at last Thy Church hath suffered and striven enough, then may the conflict issue in victory. Oh! how glorious will be the assembly of the saints, when we all as with one mouth praise Thee with inexpressible gladness! So bring us at last all thither, O Lord Jesu, where we shall behold Thee in the glory which the Father hath given Thee. Amen.

Old anon.

XXII.

Penitence.

ALL-MERCIFUL and eternal God and Father, with deep abasement and a repentant heart I come before Thy holy Face, to seek comfort and strength in the grace of Jesus Christ alone. Oh, how vain was my dream that I could earn Thy favour and win Thy heaven by my own goodness! How foolish the thought that by the purity of my conscience and my own earnest endeavours, I could be just in Thy sight! By the world, indeed, I may be praised as upright and virtuous; my life may wear the semblance of goodness in its external conduct; many an act of kindness, self-denial, fidelity to duty, may have been performed by me. But, O merciful Father, when I test myself by my inmost motives in the light of Thy Word, how different is their aspect! It was often mere self-interest, or the pressure of circumstances, or unwillingness to lose my credit and high reputation before the world, which led me to make sacrifices or perform acts that in its secret recesses my soul regarded with reluctance or aversion. It was not love to Thee, or my Saviour—not pure disinterested love to my fellow-men. The longing for reward, the eager desire for earthly credit or wealth, have dwelt deep in my heart; virtue and Christian piety have been on my lips, while my heart was full of worldly aspirations. O heavenly Father! forgive, forgive the deep self-deception, the base hypocrisy into which I have allowed myself to fall. Now I acknowledge the truth of what Thy Word says: In me, that is, in my flesh, dwelleth no good thing; for to will is present with me, but how to perform that which is good I find not. Only Thy Spirit—only Thou, my Saviour and my God—canst give me that true love without which nothing really good can be brought to pass; only Thou, that heavenly mind, which faithfully and joyfully follows Thy bidding. My own word is vain, my strength is weakness, my very virtues are wrong when they spring from self-seeking. Anxious and bewildered, I can find no rest save in Thy grace, Thy righteousness. Let me then boast of nothing but Thy merits; let me, like Paul, determine to know nothing save Christ and Him crucified; may He be to me sanctification and power and righteousness. Have pity on Thy wandering child, and leave me not till my humbled heart finds its life and solace and strength in Thy life. Thou who hast ever received sinners so gently and graciously, Thou wilt not suffer my cry to go unheeded, O Thou my Lord, my Light, my Truth, and my Salvation. Amen.

Scheibel, 1827.

XXIII.

Against Worldliness.

O GOD, my God, the Light of every mind that knows Thee, the Life of all souls who love Thee, the Strength and Confidence of those who seek Thee, grant me Thy grace that I may cleave firmly to Thee and love Thy Name above all things. My God take Thou possession of my heart, and satisfy me with Thy eternal riches, that I may cease to desire these earthly things so much. My Saviour, I am ashamed that I am so worldly at heart; my soul is grieved and pained to feel how it dwells on the things that must pass away; O Helper! help me to find my true joy in God alone.

Come, my Consoler, come, and let me behold Thee; poor and wretched is the dwelling-place of my heart, yet, Lord, transform it into a temple for Thee. It is ruinous; O build Thou its walls; it is full of impurity, yet whither can I go, to whom can I appeal, to cleanse it, save Thee alone? Cleanse me, O Lord! from my sins, and forgive my most secret faults. O merciful Lord Christ, help me to turn my heart to Thee, and to let all fleshly lusts and worldly desires go. My God, strengthen my spirit to master the flesh; strengthen my heart, not to waver between the world and Thee; let Thy grace take possession of my reason, so shall my whole being be obedient unto Thee, and all that is in me praise Thy name. My Deliverer, give me a glad and joyful mind, and raise the eyes of my soul from what is merely temporal up to Thy wisdom which is eternal and inexhaustible. My God, break every fetter which yet chains me down; let me hate what is mere show, that perisheth in the using, and care for Thee, cleave to Thee, and forsake Thee never. Amen.

St. Augustine.

XXIV.

For Courage in the Time of Trial.

LORD Christ, our faithful High-priest, Who wast tempted in all points like as we are, that Thou mightest be able to succour them that are tempted: I raise my heart and eyes and hands to Thee, for Thou art the Author and Finisher of our faith, Thou wast manifested to destroy the works of the devil. In Thee do I put my trust; to Thee do I cry; oh! let me never be confounded, let not mine enemies triumph over me. For I have to contend not with flesh and blood, but with principalities and powers, with the prince of this world who ruleth in darkness, with the spirit of evil in high places. Therefore will I put on the armour of God, the breastplate of righteousness, and gird my loins with truth, that I may be able to stand fast against the crafty assaults of the devil, and fight a good fight, and keep the field. But, above all, give me the shield of faith, wherewith I may quench the fiery darts of the wicked one, and the helmet of salvation, and the sword of the Spirit which is the Word of God, wherewith I may turn aside the evil thoughts which are secret blows from Satan. For our faith is the victory that overcometh the world.

Let no cross or trial, no sorrow of heart or strong temptation, ever draw me away from Thy word, and the saving faith; but grant me steadfastness to serve Thee faithfully in the evil day no less than in the prosperous one, to fear and love and trust Thee, to call on Thy Name, and confess Thee joyfully before the world in the time of distress and persecution. But in the time of prosperity, when all goeth well with me, then preserve me by Thy Holy Spirit in true righteousness and holiness, that I may stand fast and work out my own salvation with fear and trembling, lest I grow careless and self-confident, and fall afresh into unbelief, despair, or open wickedness.

Destroy the works of the devil, whereby he would hold me back from the goal of my blessedness, and perfect the good work which Thou hast begun in me, that I may be kept pure and blameless unto the day of Thine appearing, filled with the fruits of righteousness which Thou workest in me, to the praise and glory of God; even as it is written, 'Faithful is God who hath called you to the fellowship of His Son Jesus Christ; He shall stablish, strengthen, settle you;' and to Him be the glory and the power, for ever and ever, Amen.

Bernhardt Albrecht, 1569–1636.

XXV.

For Kindness and Gentleness in Daily Life.

OH Thou gracious, gentle, and condescending God, Thou God of Peace, Father of mercy, God of all comfort: see, I lament before Thee the evil of my heart; I acknowledge that I am too much disposed to anger, jealousy, and revenge, to ambition and pride, which often give rise to discord and bitter feelings between me and others. Too often have I thus offended and grieved both Thee, O long-suffering Father, and my fellow-men. Oh forgive me this sin, and suffer me to partake of the blessing which Thou hast promised to the peacemakers, who shall be called the children of God.

Bestow on me, O Lord, a genial spirit and unwearied forbearance; a mild, loving, patient heart; kindly looks and gestures; pleasant, cordial speech and manners in the intercourse of daily life; that I may give offence to none, nor mar the peace of my neighbours; but as much as in me lies live in charity with all men. Oh, how excellent a gift is peace! how earnestly and repeatedly did our Saviour entreat His heavenly Father, that we might be one, even as He and the Father are one!

Therefore, O Thou Supreme Love, unite our hearts in love to Thee. Soften, expand, enkindle all hard and narrow hearts. Enlighten them that they may learn quickly to forgive and forget all offences, even as Thou, in Thy great kindness, art ready to forgive and forget, and dost soon lay aside Thy just anger. Let us prize peace more highly than the gratification of our own jealousy or grudges; let us be ready to give way and yield if so we may retain and guard this precious treasure; for woe unto the country and nation, woe to the family or the individual who loses God's gift of peace! O God, resist the adversary who is the source of all discord, that he may not sow the evil seed of anger and disunion among us. Check all disturbers of peace. Scatter the people who delight in war, and bring to nought the counsels that would raise strife, and are pregnant with calamity. Let us seek peace and ensue it, O Thou King of Peace! and may that peace which passeth all understanding keep our hearts and minds in Christ Jesus our Lord. Amen.

J. Arndt, 1555-1626.

XXVI.

For a Spirit of active Sympathy.

O THOU loving and tender Father in heaven, I confess before Thee, in deep sorrow, how hard and unsympathising is my heart; how often I have sinned against my neighbour by want of compassion and tenderness; how often I have felt no true Christian pity for his trials and sorrows, have neglected to comfort, help, and visit him, and thus have stood apart in selfish isolation from my own flesh and blood. Herein I have not acted like a child of God, for I have not been merciful as our Heavenly Father is merciful; I have not remembered Christ's words of blessing, 'Blessed are the merciful, for they shall obtain mercy;' nor that sentence of the last Day, 'Depart from me, ye cursed, into everlasting fire; for I was an hungred and ye gave me no food, naked and ye clothed me not.'

O Father, forgive this heavy sin, and lay it

not to my charge. Avert from me the punishment I have justly merited; and let the tender compassion of Thy Son make amends for my hardness and coldness. Give me too a compassionate heart, quickly moved to grieve for the woes of others and to active pity for them, even as our Lord Jesus Christ beheld our poverty and hasted to help us. Give me grace ever to alleviate the crosses and difficulties of those around me, and never to add to them; teach me to be a consoler in sorrow, to take thought for the stranger, the widow, and the orphan; let my charity show itself not in words only but in deed and truth. Teach me to judge, as Thou dost, with forbearance, with much pity and indulgence; help me to avoid all unloving judgment of others, and to be anxious to moderate the sternness of strict justice by the tenderness of sympathy. For mercy rejoiceth against judgment, and Thou, O God, lovest mercy more than sacrifice. So let me put on cordial pity, kindness, humility, and patience, that I may gladly forgive, as Christ hath forgiven me. Teach me fully to recognise Thy great mercy towards me, who am so unworthy of all Thou hast done for me from my mother's womb; for Thy mercy sought me out when I lay in sin; it waiteth for me till I come to Thee; it embraces me when I come; it follows me through all the days of my life, and will at last receive me into the life eternal. Amen.

J. Arndt, 1555–1626.

XXVII.

For Strength to live a godly and temperate Life.

FULL of grief and sorrow, full of deep abasement, do I appear before Thee, the All-holy One, my Father and my God! Holy is Thy Name, pure and blameless are Thy commandments; what am I, a sinner, that I should approach Thy Face, and raise my heart unto Thee? My trembling lips cannot put into words all my weakness and wickedness; my thoughts are defiled, my whole soul is enchained by the world and its lusts; my life is full of unholiness, and sins for which I should blush; I am a slave to the charms and allurements of the world and of pleasure. And shall this body of mine become a temple of Thy Spirit, O Jesus, a member of Thy Body? Ah! where shall I find peace for my conscience; how can I dare even to pray to Thee? How often, how earnestly, how faithfully hast Thou warned me to flee earthly lusts, and live soberly and godly! How often hast Thou admonished me by the depression or shame I have felt, by sickness or weakness, by the troubling of my whole existence! Ah yes! thy punishments have followed hard upon my sins; yet with inconceivable levity have I forgotten Thy Hand; I had a thousand excuses ready; my errors, my heathenish mode of life, I wrapped up under the titles of harmless pleasure, allowable weakness; disgraceful desires I called love; Thy warnings, Thy laws I thought too hard, too strict, too melancholy. And yet, O compassionate Father and Saviour, with what long-suffering, what grace didst Thou bear with Thy wandering, disloyal, sin-stained child! O Thou Divine Love, my Saviour, my Friend, and my God! Thy heart is still open unto me, full as I am of sins and misdeeds, unworthy of Thy grace, unworthy of Thy least regard; Thou hast had pity even on the heathen, have mercy then, have mercy on me, Thy weak child; purify and sanctify my whole life. I cannot overcome; vain are my good resolutions, but Thou canst help and save, Thou canst change this earthly mind into a heavenly one. To the wounds which Thou hast borne for me, to the Love which suffered for me, does my poor, sinful, faithless heart flee for refuge. O Saviour of all compassion, Infinite Mercy, cast me not away from Thy countenance, take not Thy

Holy Spirit from me. Purify, sanctify, deliver me, O Lord; forsake me not, O forsake me not Amen.

Scheibel, 1827.

XXVIII.

Aspirations for Self-surrender.

SEARCHER of all hearts, Thou knowest my heart, and how it stands with me. Thou hast made it, Thou knowest whether I love Thee. All I am or have that has any goodness in it, I am or have alone through Thee, for it is all Thy work in me; but it must be Thine also by the free surrender of my heart. In Thy service, in proclaiming Thy Gospel, and fulfilling Thy will, I would fain spend every minute of my life. The thought of Thee shall be the sweetest to me of all thoughts; to speak of Thee the dearest and best of all I speak or hear; the joy of Thy love shall be the inmost joy of my soul. Gladly would I devote my whole being to Thee; accept me, then, as a living sacrifice, and give me the mind that was in Christ Jesus, to the glory of God the Father. Amen.

Sailer, 1751–1832.

XXIX.

Contrition.

THOU mighty, unsearchable, and holy God, Lord of all beings, Who of Thy great love to us hast in Christ revealed Thy holy Essence in our ity; I a sinful man come before Thy though I am not worthy to lift up my to Thee. I confess that I have been thful to Thy love and grace, and have ken the covenant which Thou hast made h me in my baptism, when Thou didst cept me as Thy child, and an inheritor of ernal life. Thee have I forsaken and turned y desires to the vanities of this world, and ontaminated my soul with them. I am yet unk in the sins and vanity of my corrupt flesh, and have but one little spark of the living breath of Thy Spirit in me which longs for Thy grace. I am faint and powerless; I am a wild branch in Thy vine; I have squandered my portion in the evil pleasures of this world. O God in Christ Jesus, Who didst become man for the sake of poor sinners that Thou mightest succour them, unto Thee do I haste, unto Thee I lament my need, unto Thee do I cry for aid;

for Thou art my only refuge, and there is yet a little spark of faith and trust in Thee left alive in my soul. Here I stand, poor and destitute, before Thee. I cast me at Thy feet. I call upon Thy compassion. Accept me, O Lord, in Thy death, and let my sinful life perish therein. Smite down my selfishness; slay, through Thy death, this self-love in me, that I may no longer live to myself, but unto Thee who hast died for me. O Thou rich Fountain of the Love of God, let me be buried in my Saviour's death to my vain ambitions and my sins. O Thou Breath of the mighty Love of God, fan the dim spark of Thy Spirit within me, that I may begin to hunger and thirst after Thee! Oh how powerless is my soul! Give Thou her to drink from Thy sweet fountain of living waters, that she may be awakened from her deathly lethargy. Convert Thou me, O Lord, for I cannot convert myself. Thou Conqueror over death, help me in my strife, and redeem me from the fetters of Satan. Vanquish my self-love, melt my stubborn will, break my hard heart, that I may live in Thy fear and be obedient as an instrument in Thy hands, willing only what Thou wilt. O Thou Abyss of Love, draw the desires of my soul unto

Thyself, and lead me out of death into Thy resurrection.

O God the Holy Spirit in Christ my Saviour, teach me what I should do to turn unto Thee; convert Thou my will, draw me through Christ to the Father, help me to depart from all sin and vanity, and never again to consent thereto voluntarily. Awaken in me true repentance for my sins past. Keep me in Thy cords, and never let me go away from Thee, lest the enemy once more lead me back through my own weak evil flesh and blood into the state of death.

Yes, Thou faithful God, in myself I am blind, and know not myself for vanity; even Thou art hidden from me, Who art yet so close to me. O suffer a ray of Thy grace to reach my soul. I lie before Thee like a dying man, whose life is just hovering on his lips. Quicken me, O Lord! and raise me up as a living soul. I wait upon Thy promise who hast said, 'As I live, I have no pleasure in the death of a sinner, but that he should be converted and live.' Now, therefore, I sink into the death of my Redeemer, and wait for Thee, Thy Word is Life and Truth. Amen.

Jacob Böhme, 1575–1624.

XXX.

Prayer for Faith.

O THOU gracious and merciful God, I know from Thy holy Word, that by faith alone we are saved, and that without faith it is impossible to please Thee; fain would I please Thee, fain would I know Thy salvation, and therefore am I filled with dismay, because at times there seems scarce to be any faith at all in my heart. Kindle then, O Lord, in my soul the light of living faith, that I may know Thee the only true God as Thou hast revealed Thyself in Thy Word, and may believe in Thee with my whole heart.

For there are hours when it seems to me that I cannot pray aright, and that I have no faith, or that I shall not be able to hold fast in the faith until the end. This sorrow I bring to Thee, O my God, because I know that every good gift and every perfect gift cometh down from above. Since then faith is not of ourselves, but is Thy gift, I cry unto Thee to strengthen my feeble faith. Thou wilt not break the bruised reed, nor quench the smoking flax. My God, write this comfort on my heart, that a prayer resting on the merits and death of Christ is a true prayer; and a faith, however weak, which still clings fast to God as our Father and Maker, our Redeemer and Saviour, our Sanctifier and Comforter, is a faith which Thou wilt accept and bless to our salvation. And grant me then, O Lord, if it be Thy holy will, to taste also the *blessedness* of faith, in the ardour of my devotion, in a strong consolation, and a joyful hope.

O Lord Jesus, pray for me as Thou didst for Peter, that my faith fail not; confirm me in the comfort that I am bought by Thy blood, made Thy child in baptism, and baptised into Thy Name; that my weak prayer is made pleasing unto God by Thy mighty intercession; that Thy blood was shed for *me*; that I am saved and justified by Thee.

And Thou, O Holy Spirit, bring forth in me the true fruits of faith, guide my will, sanctify and govern my soul, dwell in me, and bear witness with my spirit that I am in deed and truth a child of God. Amen.

Stark, 1680–1576.

XXXI.

For Comfort in Time of Need.

O MERCIFUL Father, Thou God of all consolation, Who comfortest the wretched, and turnest Thee to the cry of the forsaken; Thou Who refreshest the weary soul even as a cool dew the parched grass: Thou seest into what terrible distress of mind and grief of heart I have been brought, and how little relief this world can offer me; for all its consolations are now too weak to raise up my crushed and fearful heart, and give it joy again.

Give Thou me to drink from the abundance of Thy house, for with Thee are the living springs, the water of eternal life, which can save us from endless longing and exhaustion. Help me not to slight Thy consolations, nor to close my ears when Thy Word speaks to me of comfort, but that with a believing trust I may lay hold on Thy Divine sweetness, and draw from it some alleviation of my trouble. When there is nothing else in the whole world that can heal and soothe me, let Thy Word within me do it, for Thy Word can heal all wounds, and is the joy and brightness of our hearts, though we can never understand it aright till we are brought into the shadow of the cross.

Here then I tarry for Thy help. Lord! Thou wilt think on me, and quicken my soul according to Thy Word, as Thou hast promised through Thy Son when He invited all the weary and heavy-laden to come unto Him, and to find rest for their souls.

Have pity on all the desolate, who are vexed or forsaken by the world around them; draw near to them with Thy soothing love, and pour balm into their anguished souls, that they sink not beneath their troubles. Show Thy tenderness and compassion unto all who need Thy solace.

And comfort me most of all in that last hour when soul and body are utterly weak. Let me fall asleep pillowed on Thy consolations, as a child on his mother's bosom, and awaken in that place where all the faithful enjoy Thy rest and peace for evermore. Amen.

Scherertz, 1584–1639.

XXXII.

In Time of Temptation and Perplexity.

O THOU infinitely deep Compassion, Who hast revealed and offered Thyself to all men in Christ, have pity on me now, and hear my petitions! Thou knowest full well what it is that now oppresses me, and is leading me into great temptation. Unto whom can I make my complaint but unto Thee, Who wilt be entreated in time of need, and wilt gladly hear me for Thy promise sake? There is none who sympathises so deeply and tenderly with my distress as Thou, O merciful High-priest, Who hast been tempted in all points even as we are.

Ah! look on me with the eye of pity, as Thou wast beheld by Thy Father when He strengthened Thee amid the anguish of the Garden. Incline Thine ear to my cry, and cast me not away for Thy Name's sake. Help me, O Lord, or I must perish! I will not let Thee go; I cling to Thy own command, that we should seek Thy face. Hast Thou then no blessing for me? Think of the covenant and the oath that Thou hast sworn, that Thou willest not the death of a sinner? Wilt Thou snatch me away in the midst of my iniquity ere Thou hast prepared me for eternity? O spare me for a little while, that I may recover myself ere I go hence, and may yet praise Thy Name, for who shall think upon Thee in the pit?

I am indeed not worthy of Thy succour; I know that full well; but I am in the most urgent need of it, and without Thy help I must perish. Thou knowest it is so, O my Father! therefore Thou canst not look coldly on the destruction of Thy creature; Thou must needs have pity on him. Behold I pour out all my woes into Thy compassionate heart; I lay down my burden of grief at Thy feet; I cry, like the Canaanitish woman, Lord, hear me, O Lord, help me! O Lord, be gracious unto me, and let not my enemy triumph over me! O Jesu, by Thy bitter cup of suffering, Thy trembling and anguish of spirit, I pray Thee now to succour me. Help me through this dark hour. By Thy tears, and that exceeding bitter cry unto Thy Father, save me out of this death, as Thou wast saved out of death again into life. Work in me such resignation, such self-sacrifice, and surrender of my own will, that I may learn to say with Thee, from the bottom of my heart, Father, if it be possible, let this cup pass from me; yet not my will, but Thine be done!

Father, all things are possible to Thee: this I steadfastly believe; and I am sure that neither this present trial, nor any future one, shall separate me from Thy love, which is in Christ. Therefore let Thy perfect will be done in me, now and in eternity. Thou wilt do all things well. Amen.

G. Arnold, 1696.

XXXIII.

Hope in Sorrow.

LORD, when I am in sorrow I think on Thee! Ah! where else should I turn; of whom else should I think when my heart aches beneath its trials, but of Thee, my God? Never yet hast Thou let me go uncomforted from Thy Presence, then hear my prayer now, listen now to my entreaty, O my King and my God! Keep not silence when I call upon Thee, but answer me, and that right soon.

The trial I am now bearing comes from Thy hand, and Thou canst also, in Thy mercy, release me from it. Thou, Lord, killest and makest alive; Thou leadest into the depths and back to the light; Thou canst raise up and cast down; Thou liftest the poor out of the dust, and settest him among princes. Therefore I cry to

Thee in faith, Lord, help me, for Thou art Almighty to save. Thou hast said, 'When they cry unto Me I will answer; while they are yet speaking I will hear them; My heart yearns to have compassion upon them.' Listen, then, to the cry of my heart, the sorrowful complaint of my lips. Yet, O Father, I know that Thou hearest me alway, therefore I would not prescribe to Thee when and how Thy help should come. I will willingly tarry for the hour which Thou Thyself hast appointed for my relief.

Meanwhile strengthen me by Thy Holy Spirit; strengthen my faith, my hope, my trust; give me patience and resolution to bear my trouble; and let me at last behold the time when Thou wilt make me glad with Thy grace. Ah, my Father! never yet hast Thou forsaken Thy children, forsake not me. Ever dost Thou give gladness unto the sorrowful, O give it now unto me. Always dost Thou relieve the wretched, relieve me too, when and where and how Thou wilt. Unto Thy wisdom, love, and goodness, I leave it utterly. Be of good cheer then, my soul, for God will be gracious unto thee. Why art thou so cast down and so vexed within me, for I shall yet praise Him, Who is the light of my countenance and my God. Amen.

Stark, 1680–1756.

XXXIV.

Under Depression of Spirit.

I THANK Thee, O my heavenly Father, that Thou hast adopted me as Thy dear child in holy Baptism, and hast sanctified and preserved me hitherto by Thy Word. Yet now I am afflicted and weighed down by constant sadness, so deep that I cannot give vent to my melancholy, nor put it into any words; therefore I entreat Thee, O faithful God, not to forsake me; take not Thy Holy Spirit from me; hold me fast with Thy hand, that I may never sink, nor be severed from Thee. With a heavy heart do I rise in the mornings, with a troubled spirit I eat my bread, with pain and anguish of mind I lay me down again, and there is no rest in me. Ah, God! behold my grief and care. Fain would I serve Thee with a glad and cheerful countenance, but I cannot do it. However much I fight and struggle against my sadness, I am too weak for this sore conflict. Help me in my weakness, O Thou mighty God! and give me Thy Holy Spirit to refresh and comfort me in my sorrow. Amid all my fears and griefs I yet know that I am Thine in life and death, and that nothing can really part me from Thee; neither things present, nor things to come, neither trial, nor fear, nor pain. And therefore, O Lord, I will still trust in Thy grace. Thou wilt not send me away unheard. Sooner or later Thou wilt lift this burden from my heart, and put a new song in my lips; and I will praise Thy goodness, and thank and serve Thee here and for evermore. Amen.

Scherertz, 1584-1639.

XXXV.

Resignation.

MY God and Lord, unto Thee will I surrender myself, for Thou art the only Consolation of those who mourn. He whose soul abides under Thy protection, may walk in peace and without dread, for Thou holdest him with Thy right hand. Lord, whither Thou leadest I will go, for Thy ways are peace, love, and truth. Ever dost Thou guide him who trusts in Thee by Thy counsel; and though he may walk through the dark valley, yet Thy light shines within his soul and leads him safely through the night of trial. Therefore if I have but Thee for my Friend I ask no more in earth or heaven. Thou art the Comfort of all who trust Thee, the Help and Shield of all who hope in Thee. Thou art my Rock whereon I build, my Fortress wherein I may dwell in safety. O Lord my God, I am Thine, and I will never leave Thee; from Thy hand I accept all things without a murmur, for whatever Thou dost is right. Is it Thy will that I walk in darkness? Behold Thy way is good and I will praise Thee. Wilt Thou that my path be light and peace? Again I praise Thee; Thy grace orders all things, and at all times. I thank Thee, when Thou comfortest me, and I will yet sing of Thy glory when Thou sendest me trials.

Yes, my God and Father, I will thank Thee for all that Thy love and wisdom may appoint for me; whatever cometh from Thy hand shall be welcome to me, whether it be good or evil, bitter or sweet, gladness or mourning. One thing only be far from me: I entreat Thee, let me not walk in sin and unrighteousness, nor be counted among them who care not for Thee. Let my will be only Thine, then I shall fear nothing, no suffering and no death, and all things must work together for my good. Lord, keep me in Thy love and truth, comfort me with Thy light, and guide me by Thy Spirit. Amen.

Weiss, 1738–1805.

XXXVI.

Rest in God.

THEE, O Lord, Who fillest the heavens and the earth; Thee Who upholdest all things by thine ever present might; Thee, most merciful God, do I now invoke to descend into my soul, which Thou hast prepared for Thy reception by the desire which Thou hast breathed into it. Enter into it, and renew it in Thy likeness, that Thou mayest possess it and that I may have Thee as a seal upon my heart. Ere ever I cried to Thee, Thou, most Merciful, hadst called and sought me, that I might find Thee, and finding love Thee. Even so I sought and found Thee, Lord, and desire to love Thee. Increase my desire, and grant me what I ask. Bestow Thyself upon me, my God. Yield Thee unto me; see, I love Thee, but too little, strengthen my love; let love to Thee alone inflame my heart, and let the thought of Thee be all my joy. When my spirit aspires to Thee, and meditates on Thine unspeakable goodness, the burden of the flesh becomes less heavy, the tumult of thought is stilled, the weight of mortality is less oppressive. Then fain would my soul find wings, that she might rise in tireless flight ever upwards to Thy glorious throne, and there be filled with the refreshing solace that belongs to the citizens of heaven. Let my soul thus ever seek Thee, and never grow weary of seeking; for he who seeketh Thee not is miserable, and he who refuses to live to Thee is dead. Therefore, O Thou full of compassion, do I commit and commend myself unto Thee, in Whom I am, and live, and know. May my soul be occupied with Thee only. Be Thou the goal of my pilgrimage, and my rest by the way. Let my soul take refuge from the crowding turmoil of worldly thoughts beneath the shadow of Thy wings; let my heart, this sea of restless waves, find peace in Thee, O God. Thou bounteous Giver of all good gifts, give to him who is weary refreshing food; gather our distracted thoughts and powers into harmony again; and set the prisoner free. See, he stands at Thy door and knocks; be it opened to him, that he may enter with a free step, and be quickened by Thee. For Thou art the Well-spring of Life, the Light of eternal Brightness, wherein the just live who love Thee. Be it unto me according to Thy word! Amen.

St. Augustine.

XXXVII.

In Sickness.

I.

LORD Jesu Christ, Thou hast sent Thy messenger to me in the form of this sickness to admonish me to repentance. Behold, I recognise Thy gracious will; I submit and turn myself unto Thee. O my God, I too now send a messenger back to Thee, namely, my prayers and sighs; O listen to my petition, and let my sighing come before Thee. If it please Thee, my Redeemer, and is good and profitable for me that I should live, now raise me up, and grant me to live a new life in health and righteousness, unto my end. But if it please Thee not that I should live, but my end is coming now, O may it be a happy one! Come then, Lord Jesus, and receive my soul into Thy hands. Amen.

Moller, 1596.

2.

O MY heavenly Father, Thou hast suffered me to become ill, and what shall be the end of my illness? Shall I live, or die? And what wouldst Thou have me to do? My soul should wish rather to depart and be with Christ, but my flesh and blood shrink from death with dismay; and thus am I in a great strait. But I know not what Thou hast appointed concerning me; I cannot tell what is really best for me, or for those whom I love, and so I know not what to ask at Thy hands. Therefore, O Lord, I will not dictate to Thee, I will not choose for myself what shall happen. If I am to die this time, Thy will be done; I leave all things to Thee, and am content with all. Yes, Lord, I commit my way unto Thee, though it lead to the grave, and hope in Thee that Thou wilt order all things rightly. Amen.

Neumann, 1690.

3.

O MY beloved God and Father, Thou hast appointed unto me a period of suffering. I thank Thee, my God, that ere this visitation came, Thou hadst already taught me that the way of the Cross is the way to Heaven, and that even in sickness Thou wouldst do good unto our souls. I perceive well, my God, that Thou wilt now draw me away from the world, wilt make earth bitter and heaven sweet to me. I see that Thou wilt teach me to renounce ungodliness and worldly ambition, and to live soberly, righteously, and godly in this present world. Thou wilt have me prove and examine my life, and turn to Thee in hearty repentance. For when we dwell at ease and are free from trouble, we are apt to think that we are placed here only to store up wealth, to take our share in the world's amusements or her sins, to conform to her ways and modes of thought. And since we should thus reap eternal ruin and destruction to our souls, Thou dost ever from time to time lead us aside into retirement, where Thou canst speak to us alone. Ah, my God! such a time is this! Thou speakest to me now in my solitary hours. Thou biddest me be on my guard against the seductions, the vices, the habits of the world; Thou biddest me conform to them no more, but repent of my past sins, and, with a changed heart, learn to know what is the good and acceptable, yea the perfect, will of God.

Now, O my God, I will obey Thee. If Thou

permittest me to recover my health and strength, I will be more pious, pray more earnestly, strive to lay aside my former evil habits, to avoid all occasions of sin, and become a new creature; for if we love the world, the love of the Father is not in us. Complete then the good work that Thou hast begun in me, to Thy glory and my profit. Let this bitter medicine bring health to my spirit. Let me, throughout this sickness, lie in patient faith and humility at Thy feet, and find in the Cross of Christ help, counsel, comfort, and the forgiveness of my sins. Amen.

Stark, 1680-1756.

4.

ALMIGHTY and merciful God, Who art the Strength of the weak, the Healer of the sick, the Refreshment of the weary, the Comfort of the sad, the Help of the tempted, the Life of the dying, the God of patience and of all consolation; Thou knowest full well the inner weakness of our nature, how we tremble and quiver before pain, and cannot bear the cross without Thy Divine help and support. Therefore I cry to Thee in all the affliction which Thy holy will has laid upon me, that Thou wouldst keep me steadfast in faith and constant in patience. Give me grace to take Thy fatherly chastisement, with gentle spirit and a quiet heart. Give me that patience which is most needful in the time of suffering; and teach me, my God, to be still before Thee when it goes hard with me; not to receive my trial as a sign of Thy displeasure, nor to murmur against Thee in my heart, but to acknowledge that Thou dost chastise the child Thou lovest for his good. For affliction worketh patience, patience experience, experience that hope which shall not be put to shame. Help me, then, O eternal and pitying God, help me to possess my soul in patience, to maintain unshaken hope in Thee, to keep that childlike trust which feels a Father's heart hidden beneath the cross; so shall I be strengthened with power according to Thy glorious might, in all patience and long-suffering; I shall be enabled to endure pain and temptation, and, in the very depth of my suffering, to praise Thee with a joyful heart. For if we suffer here with Christ we shall also be with Him in His glory. So be it with me, my God. Amen.

Habermann, 1516–1590.

XXXVIII.

In the Prospect of Death.

I.

O THOU faithful and loving God, and Father of our dear Lord Jesus Christ, I pray Thee, from my heart, that Thou wouldst not forsake me in my need, but enlighten me with the light of Thy true knowledge, that I may thereby journey through this darkness unto Thee, the Eternal Light. O Lord, be Thou near me when I must die; stand Thou at my right hand when I must yield up my spirit; save me out of the hand of my enemy; comfort and strengthen me; keep me in the knowledge of Thee, and in strong and steadfast trust in Thy great mercy and compassion. Ah, God! may the last word of Thy dear Son upon the Cross be my last word also; that I may say with unshaken confidence and faith, 'Into Thy hands do I commend my spirit, for Thou hast redeemed me, Thou God of salvation.' And if my weakness and the severity of my illness suffer me not to speak thus with my lips, yet may my heart thus sigh and cry unto Thee in secret. Amen.

Musculus, 1514-1581.

2.

FOR Thee panteth my soul, O Lord Christ, as the hart panteth after the water-brooks. Behold I lie here, O quicken my soul; open to me the door of Thy righteousness and the gates of life, that I may enter in, and abide with Thee and praise Thee for ever. Lord, I am he who was wounded by thieves, lift me up and take me to Thy everlasting joy. I am the sheep that has gone astray, bear me on Thy shoulders to Thy flock, to the fold wherein dwell saints, patriarchs, martyrs, and all Thy chosen ones. Well I know that I am not worthy of what I am now desiring and asking; but Thou, Lord, hast deigned to receive me into the communion of Thy chosen servants, and to bestow Thy gifts upon me; therefore will I fall asleep in peace, and die willingly with Thee. Come, O blessed Lord Christ, and release me; I long to go hence with Thee; I am ready; Lord, I desire to depart, that I may come to Thee and behold Thee face to face. Amen.

Musculus, 1514–1581.

3.

STRONG Almighty God, Who art gracious and merciful, long-suffering, and of great goodness, forgiving sins and iniquities, unto Thee I cry, that Thou wouldest be pleased in Thy mercy to pardon all my sins, and to strengthen and guard my soul against all temptations. Come to my help; stand by me, that my faith fail not, my hope waver not, my love grow not cold. And when my last moment comes, let me depart in peace, since my eyes have seen Thy Salvation, which Thou hast prepared before the face of all people, to be a Light to lighten the Gentiles, and the glory of Thy people Israel. In this Saviour do I trust; in Him do I hope; let me never be confounded, for Thou art my help and my strength. Look on me with the eyes of Thy compassion, and turn to me Thy fatherly favour through Jesus Christ Thy dear Son, Who by His sufferings and death hath won eternal redemption for us.

O God, heavenly Father, Who hast created me; Lord Jesu Christ, Who hast redeemed me; Lord God, the Holy Ghost, Who hast brought me to the knowledge of my Redeemer, I pray Thee forgive me all my sins; strengthen me against all assaults of evil; shorten the pains of death; grant me a peaceful end; and give me eternal life.

O Lord Jesu Christ, Thou true Saviour, Who art the Lamb of God that taketh away the sins of the whole world, Who hast washed and cleansed me with Thy blood, have mercy on my poor soul now in its departure, and guide me into eternal life.

O eternal Life, O glorious Life, which God hath prepared for them that love Him! O glorious Life, wherein is no death, no sorrow, no pain, no fear or anguish; a Life full of blessedness, without a foe and without sin, filled with perfect love and endless day, where we shall see God face to face! Happy art thou, O my soul! how wilt thou rejoice when thou reachest heaven; how sweetly wilt thou be received there! Thou wilt dwell with thy God for ever. O Thou Fountain of Life, now shall I be refreshed with the living waters of Thy strength; now shall I depart from this vale of tears to behold Thy glory; my soul longeth after it; I thirst for Thee, Lord Jesu, my Comfort and my Joy! Let me see the day of Thy salvation, which Thou hast made that we should rejoice and be glad in it! O what a lovely day will that be which shall endure for ever! Enter, O my soul, into the joy of Thy Lord. Come, blessed Lord, and tarry not long. Amen.

Riga Prayer-book, 1707.

4.

ETERNAL God, Thou merciful and faithful Creator, behold I am standing at the gate of eternity. In a few days or hours I shall, in all likelihood, have bade farewell to this visible world; O forsake me not in this awful passage into the invisible! Be my Guide and Companion on the way to Thee! Jesu, Thou Son of David, have mercy upon me! Thou Lamb of God, which takest away the sins of the world, grant me Thy peace! Ah! open to me the gates of Paradise which were closed by sin, and admit me in Thy grace as Thou didst the penitent thief, for Thou hast the keys of death and hell.

O Jesu, let Thy sorrows enable me to enter in at the strait gate; Thy Cross make me more than conqueror! Alas! I lie here in great fear and distress, bowed down beneath Thy Hand; O loose the bonds of my sins; help me, my Deliverer, to fight a good fight, that with Thee I may freely and courageously press through death into life. O Holy Ghost, Thou highest

Comforter in time of need and even in this my utmost need, open unto me, I entreat Thee, the door of the Divine compassion. Open to me the Father's heart, whereof Thou, the Spirit of the Son, hast the keys; for when Thou openest, none can close. Suffer me to find an entrance into the true rest, and let me not be brought to shame. I know no help nor refuge in heaven or earth, but Thy pure mercy, O God my Saviour! Here let me live and die in deep contrition. Give me such faith in Thee, O Lord, that I may never see death. Amen.

Gottfried Arnold, 1696.

5.

O MERCIFUL God, Thou true heavenly Father, Thou art hastening to an end with me, and wilt speedily summon me to Thy eternal kingdom, whither I will follow Thee with hearty willingness. But as I must leave those whom I dearly love behind me in great sorrow, I entreat Thee, for the sake of my Advocate, Jesus Christ, and His precious merit, to comfort them richly in their sadness; turn not Thy fatherly heart away from them; withdraw not Thy bounteous hand; but suffer them to feel in full measure that a kind Father's hand is over them still; and, when the appointed time comes, may they follow me in peace to our true fatherland, where we shall all together praise and bless Thee without end.

Now, even as Thou gavest them to me and didst intrust them to my love, so do I give and intrust them to Thee. Thy tender Father-heart will deal better with them than we dare to think. I cast all my care and theirs upon Thee. Thou wilt care truly for them. Amen, in Jesu's Name. Amen.

Dilherr, 1604–1669.

6.

O MERCIFUL and compassionate God, help me now in my agony, at this my dying hour. O my God, Thou hast ever been my gracious God and my Helper, be so now. O Jesus, abide with me, for the day of my life is far spent, and the night is at hand. O Holy Spirit, strengthen me; keep me firm in faith to the very last; light me on the dark road into everlasting life. I die at the foot of my Saviour's Cross. To Him I live; to Him I die; in His merits I trust.

As the hart panteth after the water-brooks,

so longeth my soul after Thee, O God! I thirst for Thee the living God, when shall I come and appear before God? Christ, Thou Light of my spirit, when my eyes grow dark on earth, let Thy heavenly brightness break on my soul; go not from me when my breath is going; let me still behold Thee as Thou didst die on the Cross for me. Though I am walking through the dark valley, I will fear no evil, for Thou art with me. O abide close to me; strengthen my faith; keep me Thine own here and in eternity. I am certain that neither death nor life, nor things present nor things to come, nor height nor depth, nor any other creature, can separate us from the love of God which is in Christ Jesus. Therefore is this my last word: I rest in Him, I cling to Him; Death may part my body and soul, but cannot part my soul from Him. He is mine and I am His. I lay myself in his arms; there I live; and there I can *die*; oh! how peacefully! Amen.

Stark, 1680–1756.

XXXIX.

Heaven.

FOR the glory of Thy house longeth my spirit, O Father. Behold Thy unworthy child desires to attain to the contemplation of Thy brightness. When shall I come before Thy face; when shall I be made perfect? And shall I be worthy to tread Thy sanctuary? Thou alone, O Lord, canst open the gates unto me that lead me to Thy Light; and Thou alone canst order it, that my hope be not confounded. Oh! despise me not, but take pity on me, the work of Thy hands; help me with Thy mighty arm, O merciful Father! and let me not perish before Thy face through my sins; me whom Thou hast prepared to enter into the glory of Thy dwelling; me whom Thou hast created in Thine image.

Oh! when will that Day of joy appear, when I shall see Thee, and all my desire shall be fulfilled? My soul thirsteth for Thee, yea even for Thee, the living God; when shall I rise from this parched and barren earth to the waters of eternal salvation? when wilt Thou quench my thirst, and give me to drink before Thy face, Thou Fountain of all Life?

O fair and glorious Day, which no evening can end; where the voice of praise and gladness is heard, where joy without sorrow is known, the joy of eternity! There all is perfect, and there is nought that is contrary to Thy will. No foe, no snare can threaten more, but the highest rest, the stillest peace, and untroubled blessedness are the eternal heritage of all those who are gathered together in Thy contemplation. Oh, when shall I enter in and behold Thee? when shall it be mine to see the manifestation of Thy glory! I wait for my Saviour Jesus Christ, who shall change this vile body, and make it like unto His glorious body. I wait for my Lord, until He arise, and lead me as His guest unto the supper of His kingdom. Come, Lord, and tarry not but visit me in peace. Come, Lord Jesus, and lead me, so shall it be well with me. Lead my soul out of bondage, that she may rejoice in Thy holy Name.

Hear me, O Lord, and guide me from the troubles of this transient life into the haven of eternal bliss. Blessed are they who have overcome the perils of the stormy sea of this life, and have been found worthy to reach Thee, the sure Haven. They delight in the abundance of peace, and rejoice in Thy glory. Freed from all evil, they have reached the heritage that fadeth not away, that is laid up for us in heaven, and praise Thy grace, O God, which hath raised them unto Thy kingdom.

O Realm of light and that peace of God which passeth all understanding, where the souls of the glorified rest, and are crowned with eternal joy, and sorrow and sighing are no more; where the righteous surround Thy throne, my God, and live and reign with Thee; where Thou fillest them with the overflowing treasure of Thy goodness, and the sight of Thee quickens all their powers: O thou my fatherland, to thee I lift mine eyes from afar off; thee, my sweet home, I greet from the valley of my pilgrimage, and desire to come unto thee!

Hope of the mortal, Jesus Christ, Thou my Refuge, Thou my shining Star amid the darkness of life, guide my vessel through the billows, that the depths swallow it not up; but I may reach Thee, O Sun of Righteousness, and Thou mayest receive me on the borders of my heavenly fatherland. I cry to Thee, my only hope; I cling to the foot of Thy Cross, to Thee, Thou Saviour of all who are weary and heavy-laden. Help me and save me, and receive me into Thy hidden glory.

Oh! when I reach Thee, the Fountain of wisdom, the Light in which is no darkness, when the night vanishes at the sight of Thy countenance, then shall this longing after the Supreme Good be satisfied, for Thou Thyself art the reward of the blest. I shall know Thy truth and Thy glory, even as I am known; and shall have my portion in the joy of angels and all the blessed, in the reward of eternal life, in the riches of blessing wherewith the heavenly Jerusalem is filled. What Thou hast promised, Thou wilt perform; and recompense and reward according to Thy gracious word. Then shall I have what I sought, and what Thou hast prepared for them that love Thee, what Thou keepest for them who fear Thee and seek Thy face.

Lord, I seek Thy face and the gates of Thy kingdom, that I may enter into Thy joy and praise Thee and Thy mercy. I stand at Thy door; Thou knowest all my desire, and my sighing is not hid from Thee. Turn Thy countenance upon me, and look on me in mercy. Let me behold the fulness of grace in Thy kingdom, and receive me to Thy eternal joys. Into Thy hands I commend my spirit. Amen.

St. Augustine.

XL.

The Final Peace.

O ABYSS of wisdom and love, Who rulest all things, and appointest unto all men what is good for them, Thou only Creator, give peace to the souls of Thy servants. In Thee alone have they placed their trust, in Thee our Maker, our Former, and God. O Christ, grant Thy peace to the souls of Thy servants, among Thy saints, where is no toil, nor sorrow, nor sighing, but endless life and bliss. Amen.

Greek Church.

LIST OF AUTHORS.

THE Collects, said to belong to the 'Greek Church,' are by unknown authors, from the fifth to the ninth century; and are quoted from the 'Horologium' and 'Euchologium,' ancient prayer-books of that Church.

St. Basil the Great, a well-known Father of the Greek Church, born in 329, and died in 379, became Bishop of Neocesarea in Pontus, and was the author of several prayers, and compiler of a Liturgy still in use in the East.

St. Jerome, a Father of the Latin Church, and author of the Latin version of the Scriptures known as the Vulgate, was born in 329, and died in 420.

St. Augustine, the celebrated Bishop of Hippo, born in 354, and died in 430.

Albinus, Michael: 1624-1679. Pastor of Naumberg.

Albrecht, Bernhard: 1569–1636. A schoolmaster and clergyman of Augsburg, who suffered much persecution for the Reformed faith.

Arndt, Johann: 1555–1621. First a physician, afterwards took orders and became a celebrated preacher; author of some devotional works, the 'Garden of Paradise,' and 'True Christianity,' which obtained the widest circulation throughout Germany, and are still in use.

Arnold, Gottfried: 1665–1714. A pupil of Spener, a celebrated preacher and hymn writer of the Pietistic School; also an historian.

Böhme, Jacob: 1575–1624. The son of a peasant at Görlitz in Silesia, where he lived as a shoemaker; the author of certain famous mystical works on philosophy and religion.

Deucer, Johann. A philologist, who lived during the middle of the seventeenth century.

Dilherr, Michael: 1604–1669. Professor of theology at Nuremberg.

Eichhorn, Johann: died in 1564. Professor of philosophy and theology at Nuremberg.

Embden, Joachim: 1595–1650. Pastor at Nordhausen.

Franke, A. H.: 1663–1727. A friend of Spener, the founder of the Orphan House at Halle; a very celebrated preacher and theologian of the Pietistic School.

Gerhard, Johann: 1582–1637. Theological professor at Jena.

Habermann, Johann: 1516–1590. Author of a very favourite collection of prayers and meditations.

Lassenius, Johann: 1636–1692. Pastor and professor at Copenhagen, author of various devotional works.

Luther, Martin: 1483–1546. The great Reformer of the German Church.

Moller, Martin. Son of a stone-mason, a self-educated man, who became head preacher in Görlitz, and published a collection of prayers and hymns in 1596.

Musculus, Andreas: 1514–1581. A pupil of Luther and Melancthon; a famous controversial writer, and 'General superintendant' (equivalent to Bishop) of Brandenburg.

Neumann, Caspar: 1648–1718. Professor at Breslau, author of a work, 'The Kernel of all Prayers,' which was translated into nearly every European language.

Quirsfeld, Johann: 1642–1686. Archdeacon of Pirna.

Reiz, W. G. Pastor of Etzdorf, during the middle of the last century.

Reinhard, V. R.: 1753–1812. Professor of theology at Wittemberg; afterwards the principal preacher and Church councillor at Dresden; a voluminous author on theology and controversy.

Ritter, Melchior. Wrote about 1689.

Sailer, Michael: 1751–1832. Professor of theology at Landshut, afterwards Bishop of Ratisbon; a man of great piety and most excellent life; a leader of the national or liberal party in the Roman Catholic Church of his time.

Scheibel, J. G. Professor and pastor at Breslau; living in 1832.

Scheretz, S.: 1584–1639. An evangelical pastor at Prague, who underwent much persecution.

Scriver, C.: 1629–1693. Court chaplain at Quedlinburg; author of many religious works.

Spener, Philip: 1635–1705. The founder of the great religious revival in Germany known as the Pietistic movement; a man of remarkable piety, and a gentle, affectionate, energetic nature; he preached and taught in Strasburg, Frankfort, and Dresden.

Stark, J. F.: 1680–1756. Church councillor at Frankfort, the author of many beautiful hymns and prayers.

Storr, J. C. Court chaplain at Wurtemberg, who published a large collection of prayers in 1756.

Stolzlin, B.: 1603–1677. Pastor of Kuchheim near Ulm, during the Thirty Years' War.

Tersteegen, Gerhard: 1697–1769. A ribbon-weaver at Mühlheim on the Rhine; one of the greatest hymn-writers of Germany; the depth and wisdom of whose piety attracted crowds of persons to his cottage to receive spiritual aid and counsel; the author of several devotional works, full of calm trustful surrender to God and intense aspiration after holiness.

Weiss, S.: 1738–1805. Archdeacon of St. Nicolas at Leipsic.

Several prayers are taken from a Prayer-book published at Riga, in 1707.

LONDON: PRINTED BY
SPOTTISWOODE AND CO., NEW-STREET SQUARE
AND PARLIAMENT STREET